GW00507264

Disclaimer:

This is a work of pure fiction. Apart from Birmingham and the Law Society and types of vans and buses and other things that are real. Fiction is something made up, but it has its roots in imagination. Imagination and memories are all that we really have.
The names are not fiction, obviously, but they are certainly not associated with anyone I know who could possibly relate to the characters. The behaviours of all of the personalities aren't fiction either; I recognise myself in many of them; and you may identify yourselves with some of them too, but again, these don't belong in total to any one person in particular. If I know you well, please don't be so presumptuous to attribute any of the mannerisms to yourself. Get over yourself. I may have borrowed them. I love you. Don't sue me.

This novel was a long time in the making. I started it while working with some fabulous fresh produce and flower growers around Cape Town, South Africa, in 2006. I created the story from an idea that my very best friend (in real life) had left me her husband in her Will. The rest I made up.

MY BEST FRIEND'S HUSBAND

ISBN 978-1-8383783-0-1

Published by SK Nicholson.

Cover artwork by Claire Harrington

Printed in the UK by Print2Demand Ltd

MY BEST FRIEND'S HUSBAND

With so much love and thanks to:

My son, Ned Stubbings, loved beyond any written or spoken word (I send them in whispers across the stars to you). While you may never have read the *Teddy Ruckso* stories I wrote for you when you were a serving soldier, they distracted me when I was writing them, hopefully you understood the massive depth of my love for you. They will be ready for my first grandson, Jesse, for when he is ready to receive them. You are my *Ruckso*.

My daughter Plum Stubbings for being the girl I still want to be. Strong, bold, beautiful, courageous, independent, fabulously Taurean, hilariously funny and so many things besides that – don't ever forget the *Dilys Dog* stories, you knew all along they were really mine (and hers) love letters to you. We both missed you so very much. I miss you still. I really wish that you lived next door to me.

Emily Stubbings, please remember that you promised to be my mum in the next reincarnation. Thank you for being you. I love you.

Lizzie Norman, excuse me! I miss you! Love you loads babe.

With love to my own funny and very smart mother who encouraged my reading and madness from a very early age – my structured education got in the way of everything fun. And to my dad who possibly is the kindest person I know. If only he knew. I wished I'd known this earlier.

Additional big thanks for your support goes to:

Christine and Ian Murray-Watson, a quantum thanks (did I get that right?), for your kindness, and cake.

My big sister, Janet, remember the family game?

Kim and Ade Waite, I really do envy you.

My beautiful Barclays girls – Gill, Jax and Loz.

Ken Irving, my IB guru.

Evelyn and Rosemary – thank you both for fixing my wonky spine.

Wicks of Water Orton, thanks Donna! The BEST candles!!

And the very last word to Marcia Rathbone – It's a *Given*. I owe you.

LIMITED FIRST EDITION FEBRUARY 2021

Dedicated to my grandson, Jesse Oliver Stubbings.

Boy, do you make my heart sing X

Visualise, if you have a moment, being left your best friend's husband in her Will. Now imagine you have absolutely nothing in common, you don't really even like each other that much; but if you refuse to adhere to the wishes of the benefactor, and within her mad timeframe, then something dreadful must be revealed and everything you created about yourselves will be turned upside-down.

Forward from *A Stitch in Time*, reproduced with kind permission, from Ian Murray-Watson directly:

(ISBN 978-1 78589-156-4)

It is a truth universally acknowledged that everything starts somewhere. But that's surely not right, is it? Whatever starting point you choose, isn't there always something else before?

MY BEST FRIEND'S HUSBAND

Breaking news on every local Midlands' television and radio channels was typically delivered with inappropriate excitement about the unidentified remains of a body, thought to have been a man, found in a partially burnt-out van adjacent to an inner-city primary school.

This school was most recently targeted by parents objecting to same-sex, diversity and inclusivity educational lessons and was currently shut down. The police have said that whilst they are treating this death as suspicious, they have nothing to suggest that the location is deliberate, and more details will be released once an identification has been made.

THE ACCIDENT

Susie Bennet knew what hit her. Having already had two outfit changes, four shoe fittings, staying with the first choice of diamanté-encrusted all-weather black flip-flops, showing off her freshly painted red toenails, and the up-or-down hair trials ('up' was better because the mussier it got the sexier she knew she became), Susie had fifteen minutes to make the thirty minute journey to the airport to collect her husband, who she hadn't seen in almost three weeks, after firstly delivering and setting up the Law Society's lunch, getting change for the extortionate airport car parking charges (they didn't accept *American Express* yet) and stopping for fuel. Already on that un-trustworthy and ridiculously bright icy March morning, Susie had made three false starts back to the catering unit just over a mile from her home, in the vain hope that at least one member of her useless team of four had turned up. They hadn't, so she made a second call to the local delicatessen, having already visited that morning to ensure they could put something together for the last-chance romantic dinner she had planned for that evening. Phoning ahead, but not hands-free, as was ultimately her downfall, with the order for their emergency rolls, subs and ready-made tiny wraps, mixtures of vegetarian and fish but not Coronation chicken thank you (stains), and definitely no seeds (old lawyers and false or Turkish-quality implanted teeth made this a no-no, she had discovered earlier in her catering career).

Added to the order was the mandatory three types of finely chopped salads that no-one ever touches as they are impossible to manage as finger food.

And none of the above, of course, would be costed in appropriately, they never were, but somehow *Susie's* made money. Susie always had money.

Believed to have been recently stolen, a battered, dirty-grey van, signage worn and number plate illegible, had shot up on the inside feeder-lane from the M6 northbound, by far exceeding the Smart motorway's mandatory speed limit, but still managing to evade the many spy cameras (we found out sometime afterwards). The van appeared to have to be somewhere else, fast.

The transitioned Transit, with its tinted front and back windows was totally visible in her near-side wing-mirror as Susie reached over to the passenger seat and into her huge leather bag to answer the mobile phone.

Being a good friend and a regular law-breaker, she veered slightly into the left-hand lane as she recognised the caller's id.

The grey death-machine, having built up some impressive speed on the downward decline into Birmingham, clipped the rear of her little red Caddy with a spectacular and powerful clunk.

This then spun the smaller van across the safety lane of the A38 central reservation of Spaghetti Junction and into the path of a Manchester-bound *Mega Bus*. The Caddy was a write-off and my best friend fared little better.

If Susie Bennet had reached her mobile phone in time and answered it, the insurance company may not have paid out the million pounds her life was valued at.
The missed call was from me.

THE WIDOWER

Born in a small town in North Warwickshire, the decade after the swinging sixties that he probably wouldn't have noticed anyway, Jonathan Edward Bennet began a lifelong fascination, but not a perversion you understand, with feet. The youngest child of Katherine May *née* Egan, and the only son of Alwyn Patrick Jesse Dennis Byrne, Paddy; who upon changing his surname lost most of his once-fun persona to suit the accepting English.

The welcoming signs on the affordable rental properties greeted the newlyweds to a much better future: 'No dogs, No blacks and No Irish'.

Wrong on every front, and perhaps more so when you had fought for the same King and his Country that you now wished to make your home. His young wife had asked if they could relocate from the South of Ireland as soon as he was demobilised from the British Army's bomb disposal unit. She said they needed a new start away from the subjectivity of the Catholic Church's misinterpretation of God's Word.

Their son's fascination with feet started with the redness of his mother's big toe on her left foot and the debilitating pain from the resulting bunion, forcing the hallux to twist over the next digit. He easily determined this was not due to her wearing any particular type of heel throughout her formative years, for one thing, he knew that her family were too poor as she didn't have a pair of her own shoes until she went to junior school, but more to do with a hereditary affliction of worn-out or lazy muscles that should hold the bones in the feet together.

From achieving this unique childhood aim of chiropody practice, ('what do you want to be when you grow up? Answer "chiropodist" said no-one ever') Jonathan then stumbled upon some fairly flawed, but still open to interpretation, non-scientific research that added some gravitas to his long thought-out hypothesis that he had once associated with his mother's shoes. This was that the stretch and reshape from the bunion, and the toe marks imprinted on the inside of those shoes that matched to her only other outdoor foot-ware and her indoor slippers, proves every footprint leaves a shadow footprint, and from that impression you can determine who the foot belongs to.

In the vaguely haphazard research, used only, he guessed, to fill some white area in a specialist magazine, (*Whose Corn is it Anyway?* or something) when they couldn't sell any advertising space, there was an invitation extended for experienced chiropodists, to a ground-breaking conference to be held on the East Coast of the United States of America.

The Americans had already installed all of the latest and very cutting-edge equipment in their slightly camouflaged FBI amenities which could facilitate the requirement to investigate this footprint philosophy as a potential terror threat.

Way back then, everything was classified in this way to allow for more funding, and to provide sophisticated Western weaponry to fight anyone in the pretext of terrorism, and therefore support the financing of such from the export tax on the high-risk shipments. Win win.

And as the historical reputation of the Bureau is well known in that they tend to redact their relentless habits of taking British research and claiming it as their own, the FBI were more than delighted when Mr Bennet, cutting-edge and perhaps one of the very first forensic podiatrists, flew to Washington DC, delivered an in-depth and insightful presentation, signed some confidentiality stuff in triplicate, got a huge monthly retainer, and never looked back.

At the time the over-worked paramedics had declared Susie Bennet dead, and the police had reopened that section of the motorway, Jonathan had been waiting in the arrivals lounge of BHX International Airport for just under two and a half hours. Not the record time of waiting for his wife to collect him.

Her actual never-now-going-to-be-beaten record was in the very early days of their courtship when she had forgotten all about him completely. Exhausted from his long journey from Melbourne, almost 36 hours in total, including the unnecessary delay in the United Arab Emirates, he had worked non-stop to help the Australian Secret Intelligence Service piece together a set of events culminating with Jonathan successfully completing a back-packer's foot reconstruction and bringing closure to the case.

A traveller had been murdered and left in the Outback approximately fifteen years earlier, the only remaining parts of his skeleton still intact were his feet and one hand. The hand still had the watch attached; although the time had stopped.

The feet were positioned as Jezebel's last dance with the angry dogs. Something else Jonathan wouldn't now share with Susie.

The brown vinyl satchel carrying the brown leather sandals that had brought home the murderer to the remains was found near a Monastery in Abbotsford. The hip and fun petting-zoo for the children was also a hip and fun coffee shop, providing frothy milky *babyccinos* for the children and much needed solace for their bone-weary mothers, and was adjacent to the Monastery which had recently gained a massive sinkhole.

This may have been something to do with a tributary overflowing into the scenic Yarra River, which was loved by public-school canoeists and vagrants alike, and most likely to do with the non-stop rain over New South Wales. This, incidentally, had earlier ruined the Christmas barbecues on the beaches. Maybe the sinkhole was due to the climate changes which are happily ignored by, well, everyone not called Greta really, and so perhaps happily added to with the throwaway wrapping of the imported turkey and stuffing sandwiches, and more throwaway fast-foods later, when the beach barbecues were banned again due to the heatwaves that inevitably followed. And as the indigenous and ever-present Holstein cows chewed steadily, they stood and surveyed the tatty satchel with the almost-perfect sandals still in, perhaps worthy of cud. They regurgitated the ongoing bolus of food which was carefully reviewed and re-swallowed.

This cud-evidence would have to be gathered and examined.

That task was hastily given to one of the junior Aboriginal female members of the team. Diversity and exclusivity.

The other evidence from his many victims was dumped by the car salesman across the land.

He had a penchant for racing up and down the vast country, hence his fingerprints being on the various databases that had been rigorously searched upon the discovery of the sandals.

He had made a tradition of killing white travellers only, and getting away with it, until now, strewing his collectables over various parts of Melbourne when he came home to his lucky family. The riches he appropriated from his victims' possessions, and the occasional sale of any worthwhile property had never been tracked back to the perpetrator, as the self-important leaders of Australia had yet to agree a deal with the other more up-to-date Western forces, and had so far refused their Chinese-influenced technology. More's the pity in this case.

The used-car salesman had led the police on a merry-Matilda waltz throughout the land down under and was now in the local cop shop answering questions with the help of a very buff, persuasive, and recently divorced sergeant, with tactics perhaps more suited to an English version of *Crocodile Dundee* from the 1970s.

Still, those tactics would be secretly supported by every decent person for whom the rights of the offenders are plainly beyond their own senses of right and wrong.

A partial thumbprint on the sandal matched to the murderer.

The cast Jonathan reconstructed from the imprint of the pattern from the sandals matched to that of the remains of the backpacker's skeleton foot many miles away. The killer had been caught. The remains could rest, finally.

After this much-celebrated success Jonathan had travelled home via Doha, where he had mistakenly ventured into eating the local fare, *Mach-boos*. Mostly selecting this because the only cheese sandwich on display looked dry, curly, and was ridiculously expensive, plus the lettuce wasn't representative of anything that looked even a slightly edible shade of Romaine.

As a consequence of this choice, he had suffered the effect of the local cuisine within an hour, and missed his connecting flight to Birmingham.

His shabby appearance upon arrival back in time and into England was classic and had little to do with the unnecessary delay, that of the extended journey time, or the misplaced goat and rice *Mach-boo*. What was completely typical was his absolute inability to function like a regular human being.

Even though he had suffered Susie's appalling timekeeping on many occasions, he still took advantage of her last offer to collect him.

He waited a further thirty minutes before calling his wife's mobile phone again, the third missed call, and then, eventually giving up, he got into a black cab waiting outside the terminal and went home.

A KIND OF LOVING

Iain Theo Charles Hastings, (*Itch* to his many adversaries, and he had gathered plenty of those over his long and fruitful career) had met his latest challenge at work. He was quite a bit older than her, fifteen years and three months, an acclaimed seducer, tall with broad shoulders, but still lithe. His raven-black hair, now greying round the temples, and his very presence, together with his weather-rugged face dominated by the most beautiful attentive light-green eyes, all added up nicely to form something very attractive.

While she may have been swayed by his attention and his worldly sophistication when they first crossed swords, at his ability to recant narratives, much like Alistair Cooke who used to send his *Letters from America*, he excelled at always wrapping up the punchline with the starting subject, she never really felt the rush of love or excitement. More a fascination of a brilliant mind she reminded herself often, much later.

Hastings worked very hard at maintaining his effortless outer person. He wanted to be enough of charmer so that any dog would cross a street to be patted by him. His inner person had the natural drive and ambition combined with the innate aggression required to negotiate and survive in the money world.

This ruthlessness started when he was a young stockbroker in London and was honed via the Hedge Funds, the secret Trusts, ultimately beneficially owned by the fat oil controllers in the Middle and Far East, or, more likely, the British Royal Family.

He thrived and excelled at the Triple A mortgage bad-debt consolidation schemes placed into special purpose vehicles favoured by *Enron*.

This accounting style would be mostly off-balance sheet, so other less fortunate people could pick up that interest bill and leave the debt to their very least-favourite great-grandchild.

All of these acceptable schemes were efficiently and legitimately approved by every Western government. And on from there, he went to the tax havens of other parts of the world before they relocated their vast reserves to Delaware, and fortuitously, just before they started having to publish their true accounts to any brave journalist who didn't value his or her life.

Now, Hastings was in the honest and apparently transparent corporate world of investment banking, a more tolerable position that still allowed for some legitimate insider-trading. His move via the Cayman Islands three years ago, where he wrapped up a number of his own shell companies, although keeping control of some others, managed anonymously of course, many tidy returns made there too as he took advantage of the excellent allowable tax write-offs.

Then, for some unknown reason, onto the heart of the new financial world in the Midlands.

This only added to Iain's carefully camouflaged mystery. He obviously didn't like to talk about himself very much at all.

His next wife-to-be hadn't had to work particularly hard at anything in life, it may have seemed at first glance.

She had the air of a carefree hippy in happier times gone by, although more love and light and trees than unwashed hair and mass protestations.

Holly had an easy knack for gathering information, for getting on with everyone, networking, for being open, a real genuine kid; but she had a reputation as a scrapper. She always fought on behalf of her staff. And, she remembered birthdays.

The birthday thing was more to do with her recent subject matter, star signs, (also known as the love signs, but now greatly parodied in the daily papers – "today you will meet the man of your dreams, Freddy Kruger"), than any particular memory trick, but people loved that she remembered this level of detail and that she inherently appeared to know a little about their personality traits. Which she used to her advantage of course.

Iain Hastings' intended liked to learn new things, and even though they were never in great depth, she had once said with a defensive laugh, that she was about as deep as a teaspoon, she knew a little about a lot. This was what captured his attention, eventually. During one of the many breaks in one of the relentless and pointless daily meetings at the Bank, where their departments notoriously battled each other, as is typical in the blame-games in the corporate sectors, and where they both alternated the lead attack, Holly sat directly next to Hastings, for once, and casually mentioned something about a particularly fine double-roasted coffee bean, *Sidamo*. She said that she had tried this at the local independent coffee house recently.

Coincidentally this just happened to be one of the few beans he had shipped directly from Ethiopia back in the days of legitimate commodities trading, (and the only one he continued with now, for his illegal and 'outside of other business interests'), which helped keep the cash-flowing.

And so, when Iain had finally really looked at her, as a woman and not the pain in the arse who led the team that failed the majority of his departments' potential on-boarding of new clients, costing him huge bonuses, but saving the Bank's reputation in the process, giving her the huge bonuses, he zoned in first on her obvious insecurities. Then on to her beautiful blue eyes, her automatic and ready smile unknowingly always just hovering, and the way she would chew the bright red gloss from the bottom left corner of her lip.

He made a bet with himself then that he would marry this little feisty girl.

Iain Hastings worked much harder than he ever usually had to in this game of love. At the beginning of his wonderful new challenge, he even stopped being too much involved with his other women.

He remembered dates, always turning up a few minutes early, ordering a limousine with *Dom Pérignon Rosé* champagne in the onboard fridge, glasses chilled, for when he couldn't collect her.

He sent real flowers in pottery vases, not wrapped in throwaway paper and non-recyclable plastic, and these from the local growers, and only when in season, and not forcibly grown, of course.

Holly had got very angry once, on this very subject, while they were drinking imported coffee in a café, served by illegal immigrants, about the amount of water being misdirected away from the villages in Africa to ensure the rest of the world had fresh throwaway flowers.

Over dinner in the early part of the fall and further decline of Holly's self-worth, she again reminded him of the urban but true tale about the tragedy at one of these flower farms where the water was diverted away from the villager's food crops, solely for the production of the UK's imported disposable bouquets, and about the fat controller whom the starving workers referred to as the *Pigeon Dictator*. He would fly in, shit all over them and fly out again, a little bit richer.

This fine businessman was once a colleague of Hastings' and a little story like that will always come in useful. Hastings made a note to push a particularly well-performing Hedge Fund Manager in the direction of West Africa. Madness not to really with the infrastructure already in place. What harm could a little extra investment make. And a decent return. Putting that towards a new savings accounts for her to play with some of her own investments he said, as he guided little Holly to legally making her own money.

Yellow flowers were sent to her every Friday, as he remembered one of her subject matters was the colour and meaning of flowers. Yellow meant the joy she brought to him and the friendship they shared. They symbolised the bonds of friendship. The taste of success and pride.

He fell heavily for Holly; and on a Friday in early
spring he decided she could bear his legitimate
children.

Hastings had already skilfully and slowly isolated
Holly from the other people in the anti-money-
laundering department that she headed up, without
her even appearing to notice.

A fancy lunch here, last minute so she had to cancel
longer-made plans, a quick Italian coffee there that
meant she missed another lunch appointment.

When she made the regular daily visits to her
parents' house for tea, she may have got any
number of loving texts from him, asking how long
she would be when she was part-way through the
cooking and preparation for the following day's
meals.

Or when she was trying to support her baffled
mother by sorting through her dad's wardrobe to
retie his ties in preparation for any day he chose to
wear one. Putting his pills in order into the daily
pockets of his medicine container, for them to be
tipped down the sink in anger and confusion.

She would fold away the many individual socks he
had abandoned in his hectic and bewildered quest to
get dressed, and tried to prevent him from carefully
hanging his pyjama tops up in his wardrobe to then
put one back on again within five minutes of getting
up, as his day shirt. The trousers over his pyjamas
bottoms she didn't know about, back then.

In those early stages of old-timers, she could still
make it fun for her dad.

She matched the days in the week to the colours.

'Tuesday is turquoise', his wife used to yell at the shell of the man she had once loved, helpfully holding up an emerald-green shirt, as she too was going dotty, and therefore triggered further chaos. Holly bought loud, bright and patterned nightshirts so he could try and differentiate between those and all of his old fading shades of pyjama-like blue dress shirts. Positive dementia, she had once researched. It got a lot harder with her absence.

More often than not, Holly would find a very urgent call on her voicemail that inevitably would mean she stopped spending so much time with her parents. This in itself wasn't necessarily a bad thing, as she was always in the firing line of all the projected anger from her mum. Her mother had done her very best, she told Holly at regular intervals, but it seems acceptable for everyone to offload onto those they love, even when they don't know they are loved so much.

And especially when a fraudulent therapist experiments with some misplaced memory theory after spending one evening following a thread in an online forum about bad mothers' excuses.

Nevertheless, Holly missed the last few months of her lovely dad fading away into the unforgiving world of such a cruel disease, and her mother, it seemed, would never forgive the two of them for that either.

IAIN GETS HIS WAY, HE THINKS

One particularly researched and much invested-in evening, at a newly opened hippy-chic restaurant in the Jewellery Quarter's main commercial square, which was dripping with fair-trade-is-local-trade artwork (made by the third generation immigrants no more than three miles from this chain-owned bistro who wanted to get the airfare back 'home', and sold on-line), with the brightly hand-sewn table coverings from the most remote of Nepalese villages, each telling their own family tragedies with intertwined hairy strands of three individual-primary coloured dipped-dyed wool braiding; Iain TC Hastings had mastered his narcissistic best to emulate Holly's love of vegetarian food.

He had sent for the locally produced sparkling wine (pre-ordered by the regional manager on his recommendation and chilled to a perfect 8-10 centigrade) which Holly, on more than one occasion, had mentioned she really loved. It was cheaper than the *Dom Pérignon Rosé,* and it certainly tasted like it too.

Itch ordered an extra two crates of this fine non-vintage English bubbly in preparation for being big-hearted with the other guests.

And then, to the tears of the many diner's wives, boyfriends and girlfriends, Hastings got down on one knee. With the encouragement and the noisy cheers from the movers and shakers of Birmingham he presented Holly with a Kimberley-processed, therefore validated, non-blood diamond, (the certificate valuing this non-conflict and recycled

17

crystalline form of pure carbon at circa fifty-five thousand dollars) and asked for her hand in marriage.

Having already completely isolated her from virtually everyone, and proposed so nicely and so publicly, how could she have said no?

Wooed and married within six months, a honeymoon in Cambodia where she fell in love with all of the beautiful and haunted people she came across, those carrying the scars of real past damages, minimising her own so much, and where she attempted to recreate a much more bewitching person's acting skills at the *Tomb Raider* temple, failing to make him laugh, yet again.

Holly almost faded from dengue-fever upon her return to the million-pound newly built house (on a reclaimed brownfield site not completely cleared of toxic waste) in a gated community more suited to twenty-year-old Premier League footballers, Hedge Fund managers and drug-dealing lords; the post-viral effects of the fever later perhaps contributing to her already dwindling lack of self-esteem.

The happy-ever-after facade had to crack for them both as Iain's expectations of his wife were measured on the balance-sheet with his own sense of failures (in his head only, she would tell him).

The more successful she seemed to be outside of the house, the more humiliated she had to be behind the privacy of the four walls.

The arrival of their two children two years apart meant that she could now give up her senior role in the Bank for good.

He could keep her locked away in this family home, and *Itch* would once again rise to being the number one player in his sad, diminishing, little world.
The big-nosed and big-headed sophisticated breadwinner returned to his natural ways.
He would recant his amusing anecdotes about his funny and gorgeous children to the attractive younger ladies at the Investment Bank, and they enjoyed his stories, looking at his baby photos with awe (but don't they all look the same?) and he treated them often in his attractive bone-weary way to fancy dinners in recently discovered eateries.
Cocktails after work in-between, and, in return, they kindly helped him take the extra weight off his wallet.
Show me someone who hasn't made use of an older mentor to fund their spending and conquer their own success ladder, sister, and I'll show you so many more that have.
The marriage creaked on without purpose for a few more years, until one heatwave anger-inducing clammy day in a summer that had once held such promise, and with the recent bruises on the top of her arms, her back and her left shoulder starting to fade and stain into the ones beneath, sorting through some last minute and slyly hidden shirts (to give him yet another excuse to get angry with her) Holly was in the huge laundry room, big enough to house another few families.
She had double washing machines, one for whites, the other for colours, and a state-of-the-art smart tumble drier with fragranced drying sheets,

although the lost hippy in her preferred the sweet smell of clothes dried in the fresh air, hanging them out with matching-coloured eco-rubber pegs.

When she sensed he was home early from work, Holly turned to him asking about this particular scent on his shirt, as it didn't smell like the usual fabric softener sheets, and she appeared to smile when she said she really liked it.

It may have been just plain stupidity that he had deliberately asked for more perfume to be sprayed on this shirt by a long-standing lover and much sexier version of Holly who he had shagged all weekend, but it gave him the reason he needed to get even with her.

Hastings, unexpectedly home from the Bank via his other business interests, and having tested the latest coffee commodity, uncut, was as high as a kite and didn't bother with just his fists this time.

She tried to push a barrier between them with the heavy metal electric clothes horse and it broke his nose, bruising the side of his face in the struggle, as he grabbed the newly starched and tumble dried, still perfumed, pure white shirt from her.

After punching her twice in the stomach, he was tightening the give-away scented sleeve around her throat when Susie walked in for their coffee date. If she hadn't, then perhaps the ending would have been different.

I owed her my life.

VERY BAD MANNERS

It became clear that my husband had found great comfort with Susie within just two days of him leaving our main family home. She made no attempt to hide it. In fact, I think she enjoyed telling me every little detail. Maybe to make me feel like I had done the right thing. As if it was my decision, I tried to tell her. In her mind it would have been her way of 'sharing is caring', with that little head wiggle and crafty smile she thought I didn't notice.
She certainly didn't appear the slightest bit embarrassed about either one of their actions.
'Well, you DID break his nose, Hols.' So that justifies it then.
We were sat in her bedroom that early evening, the window blinds always open to allow the neighbours to hear her many careless announcements, as well as to see her dressing up, obviously. She had no hang-ups back then, or many afterwards. Until she married the perfectly wealthy Jonathan Bennet.
The tasteless gold sateen-finished drapes were pulled wide open too for the rest of the street to observe my pain, should the curious neighbours be too far away to hear it. The cheap amber duvet cover, one colour picked out to match the curtains and to complement the many scatter cushions that were the rage back then, withered under the heat from so many well-positioned spotlights, and my complete humiliation.
Susie was doing her best to try and squeeze into the latest here-I-am and look-at-me lingerie, sexy deep red, vermillion, she said,

which apparently was one of the safe words she used during sex with a certain nameless 'rough person'. An ongoing affair.

The outfit was virtually see-through and crotchless too. It might have been purchased from the dark internet, and looked disturbing enough on the packaging, being modelled on a scrawny pubic-hair-free gender-fluid eight-year-old.

She was obviously hoping to get lucky that night (it was probably a Friday, now I think about it).

I was fascinated by Susie's untrimmed dark-blonde pubes escaping from the lacy studded lady-garden part of the under-garment and wanted to tell her she needed a hedge-trimmer. I didn't.

At one point she may have broken my pubic fascination with: 'I felt so sorry for him', and then I remember she said 'Well, I couldn't say no with THAT in my mouth!' and she laughed, and I laughed and that was that. It really was; for me.

I couldn't tell you if it carried on much past that, as there were so many others in-between the curious blow-job incident and the foot man, and I have no right to an opinion or even allow myself to feel betrayed or hurt.

And I never even bothered to question why she had a coffee date with Iain.

THE OUT-OF-BODY-CONSCIOUS THERAPIST

Harry Palmer was running early for once. She had woken up shortly after the dark depression of dawn, taken a very deep breath in to her stomach, counted to five and exhaled. That moment between taking the next breath is where you are supported by *The Universe*. She had read that somewhere recently. She may have given some fleeting but semi-serious thought to attempting an early morning walk before breakfast, trying for the ten thousand steps that were nigh on impossible. This was apparently a made-up number by a Japanese guy, high on Wasabi (she had read that somewhere too).

Instead, she lay a moment longer in her warm, king-sized bed, listening to the grunting and wheezing from out of her mother-in-law's room across the huge landing, and every morning she hoped it would be either one of theirs' last. She wondered how on earth it had come to this.

Taking another deep breath, she attempted to push herself up from her old and worn-out sticky mattress. Even when *The Universe* was supporting you, this was hard enough.

In spite of the one hundred per cent cotton-twill sale's-pitched sheets, getting out of bed after another night of hot flushes (five years now, she just could not catch a break) was something all men should experience. Just whilst we are fighting for equality, Mister.

The small print of the enthusiastic sale's pitch from her favourite TV shopping show apparently hadn't actually 'guaranteed' these sheets would give menopausal women a good night's sleep.

She knew this from the response she had received to her very stern letter, pointing her to the almost illegible tiny print on the reverse of the shipping note. Who kept those anyway? But she was sure the wording from the actual TV pitch was open to interpretation and so this remained on her very long list of things to pursue. Spoken words and written words. Very open to misunderstanding, indeed.
Harry's peroxide-to-greying unkempt hair had taken advantage of the damp night sweats and had created an impression of a ridiculous and almost phallic shape (Freudian, and flaccid, typically) on just the one side of her head. She pulled on the only dressing gown she owned, the old and comfy once-white but now stained with sadness's past, a winter fleece with a removable hood, for some reason, that had held such false hope in the early days of her marriage.
Harry manoeuvred the dirty gown over her faded *Disney* pyjamas, to cover her flabby arms and oh so many spare rolls everywhere, (she cannot bear to look at herself) and while avoiding every mirror on the long dark landing she made her way to the family bathroom, simultaneously trying not to sit on or inhale the old lady's early morning splashes, and, if all of that wasn't enough, studiously avoiding the dehydrated vintage of her own pee.
Later, in the large retro kitchen (old-fashioned and much in need of renovation) and after forcing herself to drink the pint of water with the cheapest version of the vitamin C tablets she could buy, her attempt at rehydration, she considered an over-ripe banana for breakfast.

Fibre and goodness for the fabled fruit's legendary serotonin, this actually didn't cross the blood-brain barrier so the hype was rubbish, but one of her five-a-day nonetheless, as she promised herself every weekend that the next week would be the healthy one. She instead opted for the rest of last night's salted-caramel cheesecake and persuaded herself this was indeed a single portion. It went into one bowl after all. Along with the remainder of the reduced-priced extra-thick double cream.

Her mother-in-law's cat, officially William John Clifton Haley, Bill, was already on high alert for her in the cluttered and muddy utility room he called his empire.

He was the original monster gob-shite. He didn't bring home any presents or rewards like any normal cat, should any cat ever be classed as normal, but attacked her at any given opportunity, his head poking round the corner of the kitchen to time the tripping up, spreading the supermarket-bargain cat litter all over the old Lino and leaving his stinking evidence glistening gloriously in the centre of his mouldy tray.

This morning as he washed his right paw with alarming precision, he truly did appear to be hatching his latest cunning plan, his eyes reflecting the red from her pudding bowl, and he glowered at her eating the double thick cream whilst he was still waiting to be fed. She briefly pondered on something she had recently watched about cats, that they will scrap each other viciously, temporarily hold a ceasefire while they go back to grooming, before resuming where they had left off. Her mind often worked like that. She needed a permanent ceasefire.

Harry hated the black cat with the only passion she had left, in a way that immediately rises within you without any warning. Her anger, always just bubbling at the start of the day, increased dramatically as soon as she spotted him. And even as a therapist she couldn't rationalise or un-attach from that emotion. Well, actually she could rationalise, she had read plenty of Buddhist mantras on one of the social media platforms, she just preferred to feel some emotion. Easier to hate than love.

She had a hate-hate relationship with her manipulative mother-in-law too, for very good reasons which will become clear later, but what she really despised was the smell of the extortionately expensive fishy cat food permeating her every sense when she was hungover. Which was every day. Absolutely no chance of a shower, God please no more heat, instead dousing herself with her favourite and expensive body spray liberally and everywhere, her one luxury.

She climbed into what was dictated as appropriate work clothes, by one of the many starving girls that pass as journalists these days, and published in the reliable woman-bashing women's magazines that she read and saved to reread another time. Never finding the time.

Black elasticated and high-waisted wide-leg trousers today, to disguise her own waist, which was definitely getting higher. And the wide legs to stop the chafing. She forgot her panty liner; leaking isn't just a reward of childbirth; any sneeze can catch you out.

She brushed the side of the hair which was the least offensive, thanks again Freud, the phallic side having drooped back into sagging curls.

She applied the miracle face cream, *Retinal A* anti-ageing serum, bought from the shopping channel that was always so reassuringly comforting to her in the early hours of alcohol withdrawal and the associated sleep-deprived shaking.

Firing up her trusty new laptop to double check on today's appointments, one, and that was with Mrs H, thank goodness, Harry returned to the main bathroom, pulling with organic coconut oil for ten minutes to ensure whiteness and a cavity-free set of pearlers, this actually does work, she then polished her orderly teeth with some extra white and overly expensive toothpaste. Her ivories were the only thing she took pride in these days.

She spat some mouthwash into the ancient and original avocado-coloured sink, filthy in the way only old people can achieve over many years, found a dusty pack of panty liners under her bed, applied the ever-useful cover stick, some shiny powder, (refraction to throw the light over the wrinkles thereby hiding them, said the shopping channel, should the serum not do the trick) smudged some brown eyeliner on the top lids, black mascara (rehydrated under the hot tap yesterday so good for another month at least) and her trademark bright orange lipstick.

No-one should ever know the person behind the seventies' mask.

Her soon to be ex-husband, Manlafi Sarr, was due over later that morning to collect his mother, from the garden gate as he wasn't allowed near the house, having got an injunction against her when they had first split up.

Defence tactics, he was advised by someone smarter than him, his good friend Iain Hastings (anything that she might have used against him in the money awarding part of their divorce could now not be used without some backlash on her too). This was yet another dig in her well-covered ribs.

All she had done was to store some perfectly legal chemical castrators in the fridge, liquified and ready in a syringe. She hadn't intended to use it on him, she had said.

The regular and shockingly likeable carer wasn't available today so Manlafi (Manny to his friends, never to the good doctor) would have to drop his mother at Dan's Place (no-one called it *CP Fitness*), for the free coffee and the pretext of exercise.

Exercise her resentment of her daughter-in-law's failings more than likely, but still, Dr Harry thought, that was a good enough reason to look her best.

See what you are missing Mister, her constant sad monkey-chatter said in a parody of her mother-in-law's London accent, but the old lady had had the last word a long time ago.

How had she, Doctor Harriet Palmer, successful practising psychotherapist and damn fine GP before that, before it all went very wrong, ended up married to someone so totally gorgeous and darkish, and clever and funny with a fascination for tits and cock. All on the same body.

JUST THE THERAPIST AND HOLLY

Mrs H had arrived for her session very early; as was typically her way in life. 'Punctuality Holly', her lovely father would say, 'this shows high-esteem for other people and their very valuable time'.

Dr Harriet had no self-esteem. She knew Holly was waiting in the open foyer as she could clearly see her tiny outline distorted through the streaky, many times repaired, multi-coloured, antique stained-glass window, but the invoicing was by the hour and that included all the welcoming niceties.

Plus, she hadn't had her much needed second cup of instant coffee yet.

She had been treating Mrs H for a number of years and other people may have observed that any help she could have been for Mrs H surely ought to have shown a result by now.

But therapy doesn't work like that when Harriet led it, and perhaps Mrs H had indeed become used to the mad guidance from Dr Harry and just relied on the steady indoctrination. A partnership. It seemed to be that Holly needed this reinforcement as a child needed a well-worn, unwashed comfort blanket.

And that may have been the case, once upon a time. Of course, there had been a number of occasions where they had been forced not to see each other. Hastily cancelled appointments, on both sides, and creative excuses from Holly until her bruises faded, or it was chilly enough to wear something long-sleeved, these absences for perhaps a couple of weeks at a time. The scrapes on her knuckles were harder to cover up.

The arrival of Mrs H's children also served for last-minute cancellations (all cancellations must be paid for in full, if this was due to the client). Holly felt she had failed in the 'getting the kids into a routine' chapter of the parenting guides, like so many other mums, and she couldn't really bring them with her. But then the sweet Mrs H would turn up to the next sessions with home-made cakes, some nice white wine or expensive body spray (*Chanel* 22 too! Fake, Whoa! This last one must have been an unwanted gift, up-cycling, but beggars can't be choosers and all that) as if everything was always Holly's fault, and so many apologies.

Always a people-pleaser Mrs H, diagnosed Dr Palmer happily. Quite rightly, for once.

Today though, there was just meek little Mrs H, and no visible treats.

Standing on the metal doormat in the cold, damp air, with her shoulders hunched, she was shaking uncontrollably.

She had always known she could be seen through the hideous stained-glass door but she wasn't one to challenge anything anymore. If ever.

The mascara she had applied so carefully to try and stop her from crying, was now running madly down her face and her throat, soaking into the old-fashioned, but pretty, gingham dress, and the faded shade of the gold eyeliner matching the rivulets on her pure wool white cardigan.

She was crying real tears, hot, fat tears, those you let run through your soul and out of you as the mere effort of brushing them away denies theirs and your very existence.

Breaking every one of her made-up rules, Doctor Harriet Palmer rushed to the door immediately pulling little Holly Hastings into her own lovely padded warmth, and held her tiny bones close to her for almost the whole hour.

HER FUNERAL

Three weeks after the accident and the funeral was arranged for early on a Monday morning. It was fairly well attended in spite of that. The church service was held locally to where Susie had finally experienced her vision of happy ever after. This church was said to have been rebuilt many times since the twelfth century, lots of boring, unread history available. Although why anyone would choose to stand in the cold interior and learn something that no-one else would be interested in listening to is beyond my understanding. So much real history everywhere and yet we don't bother to explore. We rely instead on the gorgeous television historian, Bettany Hughes. She could make it fun.

The vicarage adjacent to the church was now a house for multiple occupancies, and although the planning approvals had divided the community, typically, no-one had fought it. A home for multiple families. Oxymoron.

The bright start to this cold day had faded behind the fluffy white fake clouds of chemical trails, which may or may not turn to heavy rain or sand-dust from Africa.

Who even cared?

Dressed in a white shirt with perhaps a faint stripe, I couldn't clearly see from my chosen hiding place, wearing a dark blue and slightly crumpled, maybe last seasons' designer suit, showing the state-of-art purple-patterned lining, complemented with a black tie and fetchingly attractive matching woollen mittens and red nose; Jonathan, the recent widower, sat at the front of the unwelcoming church.

Susie's two surviving children, Abigail and Tommy flopped on the same row but not close to him. Her other few children were absent in bodily form due to either being miscarried or aborted, never having had their father's input identified, if known. I hope that they may all meet up again in whatever the next place is. She can defend her actions properly to them then.

Jonathan's line of work made him fairly familiar with the bereavement theory of grief working in two primary ways. The bouncing between loss-oriented and restoration–oriented processes, he would know that after the funeral he would be faced with a third and totally unfamiliar emotion – the future plans for Susie's surviving children. This was a subject that he wouldn't have given any real attention to. Well, other than they were still living in his house, for reasons unclear to him.

I perched a few pews behind the family on the opposite side of the aisle, not intending to show any support to him. After all it was Susie's daughter, Abby, who made the announcement of her death, via social media, not him, along with a photograph of the three of them, from a time they were in Blackpool with me and my two children. Not so subtly reducing the widower's role to that of the cash machine; just a spectator at his own wife's funeral.

Everything hurts. Everyone lies, some tell white lies. Some make up their past in order not to hurt others, and others enhance theirs at the expense of others. A white lie is a good lie, the God lie. In a white God's place, and I was sanctioning the lie by being there and once adoring her so very much.

Our histories had been intertwined with so many things not good. So many things not said either.

I was sitting on a well-worn shiny cushion, trying not to think about how it got so well glossed, as I perched on the hardest of seats. I wasn't crying then, I wasn't being strong, I wasn't feeling much of anything, other than the ridge of the join in the oak pew, even through the threadbare sateen, right at the crack of my arse.

I watched Jonathan for a while. He looked as though he wore the clothes that Susie would have left out for the dry cleaners, or from the look of him today, the charity bin. All he needed now was the mourning jewellery from the Victorian ages to personify him in some *Ellis Bell* masterpiece.

He married Susie just over two years ago, another world-wind romance on her part, and since then the majority of his original persona was filed away, which was probably for everyone's good. His travelling and investigating uniform, his everyday casual, (cardigans!), his important conference-speaking clothes, his throwback to another bad taste generation (imagine red velveteen wallpaper) these were all now neatly consigned to the desperate charity shops as per the reorganisation by his wife, who obviously had better tastes.

He managed to keep the wallpaper for a little while longer.

His hideous, although admittedly comfortable, favourite upright chair with the scuffed arms, originally upholstered in a fabulous sage-green *Olefin*, which really ought not to have worn out at all, was where he liked to reflect on his subject, in the quiet of his untouched reading room.

34

This was where he studied even more feet, the peculiarities of toes, and photos of footprints and these supporting shadows. Porn would have suited most men.

The chair was effectively confiscated to the garage within two weeks of Susie moving in permanently and was where my lovely dog would choose to sleep, whenever she decided to stay with them.

The garage had been one of Susie's first projects, to convert firstly into a glass corridor which would then link two of the outer buildings, these being the coal shed and the pig sty. It was a big place, and a great way to spend his money.

Jonathan's hair had to be revamped, definitely no grey, so maybe a touch of colour? As I hadn't met him right at the start of their relationship, I wouldn't like to push that point, after all, I can find plenty to dislike about him that I know to be accurate.

If Susie hadn't entered his life and brought her own style of the closest thing to sophistication that only she could, I dread to think what he would have been wearing today. But then, there wouldn't have been a today.

I wonder if he ever realised he was almost the perfect man for her. Oh yes, in public, or at least until she was safely married to him, there were so many nice words from all the understandable languages to keep him held up on the Susie scale of cloud nine. Apparently, he is a good, decent, faithful, smart, international phenomenon. And stinking rich. Objectively one could find him pleasing on the eye, Mr Bennet.

His bewitching blue eyes, usually always cold towards me, whenever I could be bothered to look at him, or when I caught him looking at me, become alive when he delivers his lectures. (Yes, I confess I may have watched the recordings of his lectures in secret, know thy foe and all of that tosh). His floppy dark hair escapes the subtle cut from the rather excellent Turkish barber he visits every three weeks or so when he is in the UK. His physique is solid, and he would wear any outfit rather well if he wasn't so unattached to appearances.

He flies around the world getting off on dead people's feet and footprints and Gandhi's famous sandals, and bangs on about leather shoes and patterns and non-leather shoes and patterns, and inspires people (dependant on Susie's latest boost of her ego) to study other people's footprints. Saddos. And he speaks the same language as she does (useful) and she was determined to get married to him. Such a pity he is so excruciatingly boring.

The sun is mutating the stained-glass formations, and the depressing music is hollering the bejesus out of the church.

I looked over at Susie's children, Abby and Tommy. Always children regardless of their age, and I can see my 'other' son's nose start to drip. Unfortunately, no hankie has been designed for the size of his sobbing, so I went over and offered him my sleeve. I then pulled him into the biggest hug, my face on his chest, and we stood there for far too long and didn't notice who was watching, and would not have cared if we had.

THE EXPERIMENTAL THERAPIST, DR PALMER, AND SUSIE

Dr Palmer really looked forward to her sessions with Mrs B. Always a joke from a meme she had seen somewhere to start the therapy. A proper defence mechanism for sure, she sniggered. Today Mrs B had two. The one about the psychiatrist who had diagnosed multiple personality disorder for his client and then charged him for group therapy, and the other: how could she tell her friend that she was imaginary?

Susie Bennet knew she was sexy. She was bold, beautiful, brassy and bright. She was also completely unable to distinguish between the real truth and her version of truth. Her borrowed memories and great imagination cheekily enhancing her many stolen anecdotes with her smutty nuances, always made her such fun at parties. She performed much better with a big crowd.

After discharging her own self-defence routines, as with all patients, at least fifteen minutes before seeing them, and retrieving her unique notes from the relative security of a fireproof safe in the loft (only vague references would be entered on the never-backed-up software, bought specifically for such a purpose as a tax write-off), Dr Palmer would listen, nod, fill in any spaces of longer than ten seconds (although this was never often the case with Susie) and maybe make a note of any repeated phrases ('so what were you feeling just before you captured that thought?').

She used her own shorthand, and the repetition methodology, more suited to military tactics, to enable the version of truth to become the actual truth. Ask the same question twenty different ways and you will get twenty different answers.

Nonetheless, when Mrs B spoke, people listened, sometimes without choice as she would override everyone else, and, let's be honest, Dr Palmer was getting paid. Big money for old rope some of the cynical may have observed. Those who would really benefit from therapy are too embarrassed to ask for it, but everyone needs someone who will listen and not judge, and maybe just accept whatever facade we wrap ourselves up in.

Close friends are the best counsellors and will always have your back, but a good therapist allows you to come to an ass-kicking conclusion yourself. Well, a trained one should do.

Dr Harry had earlier experimented with Freud and Jung, hedging her bets between doling out further medicines (which technically she could no longer do, hence the move to a different vocation) or using talking (listening) as a placebo.

Recently, after sorting through her husband's self-help books, she didn't miss that irony, she had come across a fairly new philosophy that not only do we receive our looks and illnesses from our genetic DNA and that our behaviour and personality are also inherited from our long-departed ancestors, but perhaps more importantly to this new discovery, a lot depends on your skin colour and where you are born.

This led to another tiny bit of research into *The Givens*, which occasionally was thrown out to the clients who would never bother to do any further research themselves. An old trick for this text-book therapist. Chapter by cheating chapter.

Harriet was perhaps most interested in the way Susie spoke about her 'very best friend, Holly'.

The repeated phrases of how kind and funny and meek and sweet little Holly was, and how Susie was really hoping Holly's marriage would work out, as her husband was once the seducer you know, (she knew), and how great a friend she was, and how she was always there for her anytime Susie needed her. Every part of the friendship defining Susie as the really fortunate one, every turn of phrase, every sentence reinforcing the relationship. Susie's version of the truth.

The real therapist, Bill Haley, liked to listen in on some of the client's consultations and offer his well thought-out opinions of the sessions. No matter how many times Dr Harry attempted to kick the little fucker out of the pretty, (in her own bullish opinion) but shabby, yellow-themed consultation room, approximately every five minutes during this particular session, he had found a way back in.

The psychic cat liked to rub himself up against Susie, wrapping his tail around her neck and offering his very neat arse in her general direction so she could get a much better view of it.

Thankfully, no other client endured this particular kind of attention.

Susie suffered from asthma, along with a number of general attention-seeking hypochondriacal ailments (mixed with some genuine ones) so this tender affection from Bill Haley caused a lot of attention-grabbing and exaggerated coughing and wheezing. And Susie did not sneeze like a lady.

Susie sneezed like the raucously brazen, brash, husband-stealing tart that she was, the one who got replaced by a fine and upstanding genteel lady when she met the world-renowned Jonathan Bennet.

Bill Haley, with all his glorious and superstitious blackness, was perhaps inherently a better psychologist than Harriet. Now, *that's* a given.

JONATHAN v HOLLY

I recall Jonathan once telling me that I couldn't leave a ghost footprint due to the peculiarities of my left little toe.

This was after eighteen months of not so subtly ignoring me; walking out of the side entrance of their house when I walked in the front. He once tried to walk out of the back door but had forgotten that Susie had spent a lot of his money converting the access, in a three-week period when he was out of the country, and this now just led to the enclosed kitchen garden with the only method of escape over the recently erected and newly stained six-foot fence.

To my amazement and Jonathan's credit though, he managed to spend the next couple of hours paying attention to an almost extinct apple tree, one of the few indigenous top-fruiters remaining in the United Kingdom. The same one that Susie had been trying to kill with rusty nails, bleach and butchers' knives, to make way for her future kitchen expansion plans. As a result of this intense two-hour survey, (I knew this as I was timing him) Jonathan wrote up a very detailed paper drawing an exceptionally concise and exact replica of the fruit. Admittedly these were from snapshots taken from previous summers, and as his intense forensic work involved a lot of time staring at photos and his giving life from the dead photo to the person with the recognisable feet, an apple was no challenge to him really. Jonathan happily sent the bundle, by recorded delivery, off to the Forestry and Rare Species department at DEFRA in deepest Gloucestershire.

This was picked up with some excitement by an over-qualified and therefore extremely bored administrator, Victoria Jones, a scientist with five years of training and a lot of additional field work, but the repayment of the student loan meant that she would be almost thirty-nine before she was free of this debt.

So, she chose instead to work in a paid admin role, rather than providing free labour in a laboratory, where she may have later discovered that all GM crops needed more energy and use more sunlight to produce the very toxins to keep them bug free, than any normal non-messed with seed. And the yield is a darn sight less too.

If this student wasn't a scientist who had missed out on all of the above, then perhaps the discovery of this rare breed of apple would have been consigned to the 'utter-nutter' box, along with the many letters suggesting the locally produced vodka was not distilled using locally grown grain, as promoted on the marketing, based on the number of lorries with Russian plates, driven by Russian looking men, very attractive too, judging by the photographic evidence which was faithfully included with every letter.

And also, that the *Somerset Pomona* fruit, used in the production of the local cider, was grown on land which during the Second World War was awash with anthrax.

Soil samples would have supported this but the investment in the aforementioned distilleries by the rich, local and much-loathed land owner, who called himself a humble farmer, had provided many jobs for the local people, including those Russians, and as this must be adding to the local economy somehow, he got off, carte blanche, *besplatno*, baby.

And if Victoria Jones hadn't really wanted to become a scientist, but had continued with her first love of art, having spent many a joyous hour in the inner-city galleries studying light and colour and form, in-between whiling away the rest of her time trying to get excited about the unnecessary mutilation of the sweet and intelligent white mice and their lab-rat partners in crime, then this may not have resulted in her having the opportunity of identifying the uncommon apple.

The faded fruit chart on the wall in the sub-DEFRA office was barely representative or even slightly the right *Pantone* colour accuracy when it was first printed, and indeed if anyone was to bring samples of other unique apples in the physical form into the office, the likelihood was that they would have been dismissed.

The fruit would be confiscated and very likely saved as a reward, or punishment, for the unfortunate rodents.

If all of the aforementioned had not been the case, then she may not have escalated Jonathan's excellent research and accurate artwork to her supervisory superior. Who, in turn, as he was male and therefore automatically more privy to the mandates from the *Orwellian* guide of who runs the world, was totally aware of the private funds who hold the purse-strings and therefore the cabinet department that determined his career.

He knew that this tree could create major upset in the status quo of offering more than two indigenous choices of apples to the ignorant public. Those that were grown only in government registered Kent orchards, and where the apple varieties at every supermarket of the consumers' choice was based on whether they were loose or pre-wrapped in branded plastic bags.

And as long as the shopper continued shopping from one of the major supermarket chains, who were also part of this private fund (which ultimately led up to a Trust, as no-one knows who owns us really), then everyone had the perception of freedom of choice.

It was that same supervisor, superior in every sense, who was given a hefty bonus as a thank-you from the faceless Trust for alerting them to this important information and therefore allowing them to condemn this tree and remove its very existence from the Midlands.

Victoria Jones was allowed to leave shortly after that, as funding for this area had suddenly become tight. Government cutbacks you understand. She didn't.

Had Jonathan taken more time to do some research, he would have become familiar with the many conspiracy theories, based in truth, regarding the power of the GM seed providers, those also owned by the conglomerates who determine what we eat, how it is farmed, and which non-EU country can farm it.

He would have learned how it had become mainstream and acceptable, to push the organic agenda into the middle-class ethics, when not so long ago organic was the norm.

The middle-class shoppers still used the same faceless Trust's supermarkets, so in that respect no-one really bothered.

Alas, the thorough, forensic podiatrist had only alerted the money-makers.

And whilst he ought to have been congratulated at discovering this once populous variety, after all his totally respectable paper would be used for future internal staff training, along with his artwork still displayed underground in Herefordshire, both without his knowledge or approval, Jonathan didn't have to wait too long before hearing back from the faceless governmental office that is fronted by the seemingly transparent and innocuous DEFRA.

Within two weeks of alerting the regime, this rare and beautiful tree had been lopped. Its proud and once noble stump and every shred of its existence was removed and loaded onto an anonymous flatbed truck, along with virtually all of the topsoil from the half of an acre garden as 'samples' just in case the rare and beautiful last *Greasy Pippin* dared to have the audacity of reproducing itself.

This load was to be transported back to the anthrax-ridden site in darkest Gloucestershire where, maybe, its DNA was extracted and merged with some toxins, to establish, perhaps, the former European Union's recommended GM safety record.

The saplings planted in a field to be studied next to un-messed-with crops would be watched over by a lowly student on unpaid work experience, to record the inevitable bee deaths.

Susie was delighted they had been able to get rid of the tree without paying for it, as it meant the extension could go ahead and the land was now clear for decking at no extra labour costs to them.

Jonathan was confused as he had hoped that DEFRA would embrace an almost extinct fruit tree.

I was beyond angry at how stupid Susie was and that Jonathan, for one so gifted, was so staggeringly naive.

STILL THE MOURNING

Jonathan finally notices Tommy is crying his own kind of cry. He was taller than Jonathan when Susie took over his life, and he doesn't seem to have shrunk much at all. He briefly considered going over to him but chose to stay away.

He had wondered what would happen to Susie's children, but that was always something to deal with later. For now, he just needed to observe everything. Holly had gone over to Tommy. She made him smile, she can always do that, probably at someone else's expense. Jonathan doesn't think he likes her.

Not because she made Tommy smile, but because she really could not be as smart as Susie had said she was.

She's not particularly pretty and certainly doesn't have the in-your-face persona that Susie has. Had. Holly is, well, just average.

Susie told her husband that before she met him, Holly and her would drink cheap wine, but never go out partying or to the bars in town. Susie went out with all the other usual suspects, the ones she didn't keep from him; she thinks we don't have pasts. It was almost as though those two didn't need anyone else in their lives.

He knew they were separated from their respective husbands within a few months of each other. Holly's left her following something that Jonathan didn't pay too much attention to, a fight maybe, and Susie's marriage ended as her husband was unable to keep faithful, she said. How about that.

Susie's ex-husband, the hapless small and weak father of her hopeless children, she used to say.

They got the majority of their looks from their mother, she said. Thank goodness, she added. He's here too. She had one before him, and Jonathan was the next in line.

'Hey Andrew'. He heard Holly talking to the second husband and father of the two survivors, and observes as she drags Susie's still sobbing son over to the open grave.

They all watch his dad as he threw a bunch of hand-tied flowers into the open grave; Susie's favourite, purple *Sweet Peas*, out of season in the UK obviously and so locally imported from Holland. The straw ribbon broke and the flowers scattered across the top of the non-eco-friendly wooden coffin. (Beautiful flowers to look at but don't eat the seeds as they contain mildly poisonous *lathyrogens*).

Even in death, Susie's true nature was quietly continuing to be unfurled.

Holly remembered only then that Andrew had called her a few weeks ago (he left a message on her answering service, as she very rarely got to the phone on time) and said of the problems his new wife was having with conceiving, and she really had meant to follow this up, after momentarily wondering why he had shared this.

Susie's death had put paid to many things. Holly hadn't called him back.

Maybe they were all expecting Andrew had come today to support his children and take them back with him to a more familiar situation, to make their new home at the smaller house with his clever wife of three years.

But the mourners, her new spiteful village friends, suspected he was probably there more to show his respects for the free food and drink, and weren't the kids better off in their familiar environment?

Susie told everyone everything. No dignity ever spared and sometimes a smattering of truth mixed with her many lies. Jonathan made no effort to go over to him and Andrew followed this excellent example.

People were starting to move away from the hole in the ground.

The vicar, who had never met Susie and therefore didn't know her, had delivered a very dreary and standard sermon about ashes and stuff and was hurrying the mourners away as yet another grieving family were due shortly. Death waits for no man.

The Eulogy was written and performed with a few inappropriate remarks by Daniella Ingle, a new friend into the fold and, perhaps tellingly, to some in the know, never all three ladies together at the same time.

Friend one-up-man-ship. Daniella gave a brief overview about when and how they met (which surprised Holly). She told of the many scrapes they managed to get out of, probably made-up stories from Susie's inherited memories but it was still funny and poignant, and brought a lot of laughs and a lot of tears.

But mostly, the congregation were quiet.

Perhaps due to watching this fabulous creation and her insanely elegant black dress and the trademark funeral Cowboy boots and crazy pink neck scarf, (to hide the fading scar from her Adam's apple surgery) rather than out of the required respect for the occasion. Daniella had said about how one day we will die but all the rest we will live, so let's choose to live.

We'd all read that motto somewhere on social media, but still, no-one really thinks about death as something that will happen to them just yet.

Maybe we are all perfect *Straw Men* in the big wheel of life, and death, where the more tax we churn out the more profit we make for others.

Take the coach driver on that fateful day. No-one remembers his name. There was a schedule he had to keep to, he had a lovely and loving family to feed, and late pick-ups resulted in docked pay, regardless of other mitigating factors like, say, traffic. People had booked online and for their two-pound fee and slightly shocking admin charge (still cheaper than letting the train take the strain) they expected to be picked up from the allocated bus stops on time, and that day they were.

Unfortunately for Susie. Her death equates to nothing. Nada.

There were two people on the coach. Eight pounds plus that booking fee and the card charges that the public are unaware of (*American Express* will do nicely sir, extortionate fees). Subsidised death.

Dear, lovely Susie Bennet. Confidante, conscience, pillow talker, surface-perfect lady.

The people on the bus didn't even know her. They didn't know her sandwich run, her many secrets, her cruelty, nor her manipulative ways that were dressed up in self-serving and very public displays of kindness.

The people on the bus also didn't know that the driver, not only suffering from the shock of being behind the wheel of the vehicle that crushed the Caddy, had also lost his job to boot, they said 'careless driving', and after committing suicide he would later lose the love and respect of his family, as they had to move on without him. Just another number.

Holly left Tommy with his dad at the grave, making them pinky-promise not to fall in; and then after taking some time to herself, she finally walked over to Jonathan giving him her best smile as she said: 'We've got to get this lot fed and watered. Do you want to meet and greet back at the pub or shall we sidle in through the tradesman's entrance?'

Jonathan tried to give the impression of something, maybe interest or genuine dejection, as he focused on her wonky teeth for a while and then replied: 'As I am not sure of what I want to do, Holly, I would prefer not to expose the wrong emotion.'

Which was so bloody typical of him. Her anger rising but consciously choosing not to make a scene on this day of all days, she instead calmly invited him to gather up the kids post-haste, and at least pretend to care.

And through her frustrated tears Holly stood back, watching him trying to put on a show of functioning, concern or even noticing the children at all, as they fell into the unconscious gloom of the long, black, funeral car.

Disappearing, one by one.

And as she saw husband number two follow the throng back to the waiting cars, no doubt hoping for some words of comfort for his own sense of bewilderment, she may have cried to myself 'Oh Susie, I'd do anything to bring you back. Send me advice and guidance and I will take it, I promise.'
But Susie, somewhere between the disturbed earth and whatever version of heaven was waiting for her, kept quiet.
Unusual in itself, but appropriate, given the circumstances.

SUSIE, LAID BARE

I recall an afternoon one summer while sunbathing in Susie's lovely, lush back garden (no hosepipe bans ever applied to her) where the shrubs, like her children, competed with each other for light and attention, giving the wild flowers no chance of survival. This was long before she had met and manipulated Jonathan into marrying her, and when she told me about being abused by her mother's husband.

Susie always sunbathed naked in the relative safety of her overgrown back garden, sometimes just to wind the neighbour up (a few days after one of these unclad sessions he somehow forced his way into her garden and raped her, but this wasn't reported to the police, or mentioned to his plain wife, just another notch she didn't want to include on her very etched headboard), but mostly she sunbathed like this for an even tan. For a naturally blonde girl with the fairest of skin, that would now never wrinkle, she baked to a lovely bronze.

'Abused?' she turned to me allowing a good glimpse of baking bosom. 'From the minute that bastard married mum.' She laid down again, settling her curves into position. 'The sun didn't shine in those days' she said. 'I hate the sound of opening doors.' Of course, there's a fascination. We don't like to mention that we need to know all of the details, but we might pay to watch, and perhaps nearly all of us have slowed down, rubbernecking, as we pass an accident. After the first few months of confession, 'offloading', Susie had said, with a wink, she didn't mention the abuse to me again.

She never appeared to warm to the Birmingham-born Anglo-Welsh-borders' stepfather, who liked to think he wasn't a Brummie due to his parent's heritage, but the slipping into his Welsh accent had him sounding as though he was a native of Pakistan. Think more Lahore than Llandrindod Wells.

This made for even more comedy after he had a stroke later in his life. No-one went to visit him at the end. A small, belated victory for Susie.

For some unfathomable reason though, Susie would always ensure that she played the perfect hostess to him. Birthday parties for her lovely, uneducated and failing mum. Having everyone round for Easter lunches and Christmas dinners, Susie would graciously accept the very generous handouts from her first abuser on behalf of her children.

Those handouts he made with very public and uncomfortable gestures of affection to Abby and Tommy, whilst so obviously drooling over Susie's fabulous chest, which was always on display.

If I had asked my therapist her opinion she may have said 'perhaps he was assuaging any guilt'.

But I hadn't, and on looking back I think there was a display of dominance which had become both instilled in her and what drove her to seek solace, with just about any man. What did I know.

I got to hear many stories over that summer, and I now accept that these were probably a mixture of some things she had watched on television and some genuine horror tragedies from the headlines on the daily papers.

These may have included some other made-up stuff, possibly including the pseudo-Welshman, which became more credible over the many repeated tellings.

And back then, I offered her my ear, some half-decent Australian wine (more than likely blended, as it was still very cheap) and what I now hope was true friendship. Defending her behaviour when it was beyond indefensible, supporting her through her many twenty-four-hour breakdowns, and wiping her tears when the next man of her dreams left after the one-night stand and never returned her calls.

She married three times. The first to get away from her mother and the abuser, at the tender age of eighteen. This particular bad-choice stole her weekly pay packet and would lock her indoors whilst he impressed other girls with his newly-found wealth. The second one was to get away from the first. Andrew just happened to be the then-husband of a very good friend of hers, and was the father of her children (the first child out of wedlock).

The third marriage was to Jonathan, because she said she had finally found her soul mate. Someone who was well outside of the vast area of flattened grass more likely.

Susie had been bringing up the two children on her own since they were pre-school and Andrew had left. She worked many jobs and slept with many men.

'I've got a thing going with BB Brad' she told me one morning after once again having forgotten to collect her kids from mine the night before.

(BB Brad was a neighbour who thought he looked like Brad Pitt's brother and 'popped' quickly, hence the ball-bearing gun reference. Hers obviously).

I mentioned his marital status to Susie as there should be some rules, maybe not always a visible wedding ring, but certainly not another friend's husband of over ten years with absolutely no previous history of extra-marital activity. His wife was the sweetest and kindest cripple who we all knew had found some special ways of keeping her husband satisfied.

'He needs the real thing' Susie explained, as though this was a huge favour she was bestowing on Mrs Ball Bearing. And that was Susie.

Her head and morals worked differently to virtually any other woman I have ever met. It was almost an act of kindness, her giving it up so easily, and maybe, for her, that was close to the truth.

This led to BB being loaded and popped every Tuesday night after she'd finished one of her three jobs, this particular one as the late-night shelf-stacker at the local wine merchants. Other people noticed he would stay behind after his weekly purchase of one bottle of red wine, the cheapest, Spanish, and then offer her a lift. And other people liked to talk. I don't want to believe that their interests were satisfied by the outrageous sex displays beyond the always open curtains, but for a long while Susie's three storey end terraced house at the bottom of the cul-de-sac was the spectator centre of the once suburban village.

I remember the year we took our children out of their junior schools one Friday in early October to go to Blackpool to see the *Golden Mile* lights.

Somehow the donkeys were still forlornly waiting on the sands, carrying on their rides within acceptable abuse guidelines.

These fine and underrated members of the *equidae* family never seemed to complain, although you only had to look at the tears in their eyes to see the torment. The hypocrite in me allowed the children to partake. We all ate tooth-rotting candy floss in the afternoons and fish and chips on the famously windy promenade in the evenings.

The Saturday night Susie had managed to persuade the owner of the B&B to baby-sit for us 'as we needed a break from the children', hers obviously, and we hit the bright lights of the wonderfully cheap pubs. I ended up holding her tacky fake designer handbag for a full fifteen minutes whilst she experienced some stag-weekend tripper in the Gent's loo, although I wouldn't swear he was part of any party. Just another lucky guy.

Susie fell in love many times. Sometimes the affairs lasted all the way through to the morning and sometimes we got into days. I watched my friend on self-destruct, showing no signs of it. If I raised the subject of her latest conquest, she would either refer to his sexual abilities (and wow did I learn so much) or that the colour of his shirt was wrong, and the most telling of all, she knew the surname.

If we got to the surname stage early on, then the heartache of them not calling her was all the greater. This time last month Susie and I had shared some decent wine, for once, as I had brought it round.

She had an eye for the bargain bins wines, and back then I was still at the stage of valuing my internal organs.

I had stayed at their lovely converted cottage in their sunroom, she had extended over the *Greasy Pippin* hallowed ground by then, and I was on my own designer camp bed. Susie had bought it for me.

She loved being married and pretended to miss her other party friends, but I don't think she saw so much of them now.

I was perhaps the only friend who was allowed an all-night stop over with her and mostly only when Jonathan was out of the country, so she could tell me all about his failings it seemed.

Looking back now, I realise the timing was indeed deliberate, and maybe I had suspected it then, but I just put it down to careless speak after alcohol.

Things that Susie wouldn't ever want him to know, and as if I would have told him.

Even if I could have remembered.

THE EXISTENTIAL THERAPIST AND SUSIE

Dr Harry had recently taken to blasting her many varied play-lists very loudly before and after the sessions with Susie. Cleansing music therapy for the soul, she affirmed to herself as she danced around the neglected kitchen, avoiding the manic cat and bouncing and bruising off the cluttered work surfaces. She had invested in a very easy to operate Blue-Tooth speaker that you could even clap on and off. Another bonus, or a side effect according to the small print (that no-one ever reads) was that apparently it could interfere with cats' behaviours by funnelling high-pitched waves through their pinna's and she took advantage by experimenting with this newly-found joy. Nothing to report yet. And she wouldn't have cared.

Any other medical expert, or even a regular, normal person, would have clearly said that the music could sway the lines of support to suit the therapist and not the client, (with the focus on the word 'could', as every therapist's rule number one is to not allow themselves to influence end behaviour. So the inference was clear – just don't do it). But Dr Harry was totally self-assured in her own area of expertise to know this wasn't the case for her. It was her newly discovered way of putting herself in her bubble, rather than preparing correctly for her client.

Afterwards it was to rid herself of anything that may have affected her during the session.

She needed a lot of loud music these days. Music is known for its many healing properties.

As the reliable Bible says; it is better for a man to hear the rebuke of the wise than to hear the song of fools. *Ecclesiastes.*

On the morning of Mrs B's appointment, not only had she heard the distant siren songs from the local fire brigade's test run (and thought about her client and the hilarious recollection of her two-date relationship with one of the crew, Fireman Pam, so called as he loved dressing in Susie's crotchless cami-knickers, another laugh out loud story. Susie didn't hide her many conquests to anyone other than her new husband) but the play-list started with the now dead artist who had become a symbol.

As Harriet opened the door to Susie the words 'alone in a world that's so cold' kept playing on repeat in her head. And she felt it. No-one would ever have called *Prince* a fool.

'Susie' said the good doctor, 'hi, come in.' And Susie quietly did as requested.

Afterwards, and trawling through the illegible session notes, Dr Harriet may have noted references to secrets (nothing new there), children (a surprise as she was never going to be writing a manual about child rearing, unless Dr Spock co-authored it), Dr Harry allowed herself a snigger at that thought.

Also in the jottings were more comments on Susie's friend Holly and whether she could handle the truth (she allowed herself another snort at that film reference).

If Harriet Palmer hadn't been such a functioning alcoholic (which may have been another reason for hasty retirement from general practice, not just her husband being caught in the local public lavatories so many times) and her brain cells hadn't almost depleted to the point beyond severe memory loss and brain fog, then she could have joined the dots. As a good therapist is trained to.

She could have guided the sessions to help her clients see, if not the error of their ways (in Susie's sessions for sure) to try and help them get to their own conclusion without it being forced. Therapy should not be used as a sledgehammer.

Those afore-mentioned dots and notations would then support the inkling that she had (although inklings are not acceptable in a court of law – facts only dear) of Susie's not-so-secret big secret.

All the signs were there, and they certainly were not going anywhere.

Alas, a good therapist may have been trained in a range of treatments, and qualified as such to become a specialist, but Dr Harry had relied solely on her medical certifications.

She hadn't bothered taking any further formal training outside of the regulations required to dole out medicine or placebos.

She nursed a huge crush on Carl Jung, (who hasn't?) and had spent some time looking at the existential *The Givens*, something more New Age than traditionally accepted in her opinion, and if she was going to bother to go down one particular avenue of therapy it ought to be that one – but by the very nature of existentialism then it would be outside of innate behaviour, and she didn't miss the irony there.

So, instead, Harriet bought the occasional self-help book or monthly mind magazine from the corner shop, and these became part of her armoury. Her useful dip-in and dip-out tools to support whichever philosopher or therapist who was her choice of the season, any season.

This particular session started not in the usual way of Susie sharing a joke or declaring her latest battle, or hardship, or borrowed behaviour from whomever she had encountered recently, but more a melancholic Susie, who matched her mood to her sombre clothing. Tits still out though.

These words may have been tinged with some regret. Deep breaths that judder on the way out. Certainly not the usual version of Susie at all, as she asked: 'What's the worst thing you can do to another person, short of torturing them by a thousand cuts or killing their children?'

There was little point in Dr Harry nodding or adding anything, as Susie didn't ever need any prompting, and she wasn't even looking at her therapist anyway.

'And to such a sweet little girl, who I made sure became my friend outside of nursery school that day. And to be such a horrible person. What will happen if it all comes out?'

And with no surprise, as was so typical for Susie, she asked: 'who will be my best friend then?'

WHERE THERE'S A WILL

It was possibly just over a week after the funeral that I got the first contact from Jonathan. My days and weeks had tumbled into each other long before Susie had died.

'Holly', he said, when I finally took the call. This being after he had attempted three times to get hold of me (why don't people just leave me a voicemail then I can decide whether I want to talk to them?). There wasn't any 'hi' or 'how are you' or 'thanks for everything you did at the funeral', instead he said:

'It appears Susie has left a Will and your presence is required as you are mentioned.'

I laughed out loud and asked him if she's left me her children. 'And don't tell me she left me that hideous awful fur coat either' I added.

But, as was so bloody typical of him, he didn't acknowledge either comment, just gave me a time and a date for the following Tuesday, and without asking me if that was suitable, or how I was, or if I had any indication about this Will, or anything really that a normal person would do, he hung up without saying goodbye.

In completely bad taste, but something that would really have appealed to Susie, our Will reading was at the same Law Society's office that she was on her way to on the day she died.

I wondered if they knew the lunches they paid through the nose for, tended not to be the creation from *Susie's* (previously named *Susie's Eats*, but after blowing my husband, and many other people's husbands before that, I advised her to remove the *Eats*).

63

She usually picked these up from the Deli local to her catering unit. Her staff were unreliable and she never had the same amount of time in a day that the rest of us monotonously crawl through. Not enough hours in the day now anyway.

Susie had always said she didn't particularly like this bunch of people, even though they had been clients for many years, maybe even her first client. And so it was odd that she made a Will and had chosen this lot.

If you had known her, and I really wish that you had, you would clock that she was a master in the adding-up department, could knock off a round of sandwiches at serious speed, when not using the back-up Deli, and she could cost-account faster than any of the big four accountancy partnerships, and more accurately too, judging by their recent results. But as for a Will that her husband wasn't aware of, this just didn't fit with her behaviour. Susie shared everything, real and make-believe, with everyone.

I caught up with Jonathan in the stuffy reception area of the Will-reading room (yes, such a thing exists) which in itself was impressive enough to be described in loads of fabulous detail as would befit any *Agatha Christie* novel.

The ancient and restored original wood-panelling was circa the 18 Century, I read on the faded little plaque, the appropriate wall coverings – pictures of wankers in red coats hunting the desperate foxes, and some other pointless fabric things.

And as I took in the opulent misdirected wealth and smell of proper leather polish (tanneries and too poor to have a pot to piss in came to mind),

I could think only of the misery of the poor cow that had died to give her unborn calf's soft leather for the many unappreciative fat behinds that bounced and sweated on the expensive couch, while waiting to see what they may inherit from people they didn't even think about when they were alive. It was that sort of place, bringing out the worst in me for the sniff of money.

I managed to find a chair that was covered in something other than leather, just to make a point. Obviously, no-one had sat in it for a few years as the loud and rather rude rumpus that shot out from under me when I plonked down made for a spectacular display of dust mites rocketing out in every direction and hovering in the weak city sunlight. More than enough dust to set us both off sneezing, but Jonathan, clearly unperturbed by this, was muttering something along the lines of 'I didn't know she had a Will; it must have preceded the one we drew up together before we married. But we did that with my own solicitors, surely, they have the latest. They must have the latest, doesn't marriage override these things.'

I didn't reply as I couldn't be bothered to, and was too busy brushing the small particles along with the embarrassment from my arse. I was only half-listening to be honest, but also didn't add anything because I wasn't sure if any comments were needed; and I didn't know how I was feeling about being here. I don't know that I was even capable of knowing how I was feeling, but then I never did.

I'd tried to explore this with Dr Harry, this lack of any emotion, but suspected she'd never got to that paragraph in her *Psychology* magazine. Note to self: why am I still seeing her?

There was a slight tap at the entrance to the room and the door opened up to a very solemn-looking solicitor, another appropriate suit – just what is it with playing a role – when did we get stamped with yet another *Straw Man* personality, a name, a national insurance number, the chosen career and taxable earnings that would then define us for the rest of our lives? He introduced himself and I caught a glimmer of recognition at his name, Samuel Hillary. One of her old flames maybe? He also noticed me looking at him with the same recollection reflected in his shiny, foreign-sun tanned and botox'd face, but as I couldn't recall enough, I decided to let him off. After all he was loaded with the appropriate legalese and Latin-speaking documents, looking important in the way that only the nouveaux riche with their polished-turd-leathered heads can pull off, and this was, nonetheless, no time for frivolity.

I made myself another mental note, this one I immediately let go, to ask Jonathan if these solicitors had sent a sympathy card and, come to think of it – how did they even know she was dead? I reminded myself to refrain from asking if the same collective investment firm that was the senior partner, and therefore significant controller of this limited liability partnership, had subsidised any failing coach services recently.

I already knew the answer to that. Old investigation habits died hard, as I'd somehow managed to keep my links to the Bank's systems.

Well, I'd kept Iain's.

I listened to the solicitor's dramatic throat clearing, wondering if the dust had got to him too, as he took a huge gulp of water from a fancy cut glass bottle via a fancier crystal glass and then he started to read.

What did he just say?

Jonathan looked over at me as I roared with laughter. Did he just say what I think he said? I glanced over at Jonathan while wiping my tears away with the stiff paper–coaster from the fancy water bottle, but he isn't laughing – just what in the name of Sam Hill is actually wrong with him?

'I knew she'd find a way to leave me her kids' I said. Hardly able to breathe, I was snorting through the dust and my happy tears.

'This is her way of making sure we support each other and so we don't mourn her. The fun side Jonathan, this is so Susie, I love it!'

The solicitor had said something about a twelve-month timeframe, and that Susie had come to him in all seriousness, just under four months before.

She had made this new Will and Testament whilst of sound mind, yeah right, stipulating that if she died while she was still happily married to Jonathan, that her final wish was for her best husband and best friend to get married.

Within a twelve-month period from the date of the reading.

By now, Jonathan had the look of the cartoon cat that got hit with the frying pan whilst walking off the edge of the cliff, and worryingly appeared to have stopped functioning.

Jonathan, with his usual dull and stiff manner
matching his usual monotonous and shabby clothing
(today he was mostly wearing black trousers,
matching suit jacket and off-white shirt – it looked
like it had been washed with something red, why do I
care so much?) turned to look at me, almost
weighing me up in his scientific manner, working out
the Susie versus Holly balance-sheet calculation.
He didn't laugh either when I said: 'And I'm not
having her kids either – they have their own dad,
thank you.'
And in my mind, I'm saying to Susie 'Forget the
marriage chick, it may have worked for you both and
I know you wanted me to have your fake pseudo-
happy marriage, yes babe, I know he almost fitted
your lets-pretend happy-ever-after make-believe
world. You told me often enough.
'You, Susie, settled for someone because he was
more or less suitable. You had a big spending habit
and he had money, lots of it. Yes of course I was
aware of your working arrangement. I may have
envied your way with each other. I loved your
organisation skills that gave him just the right
amount of attention when he was around; the way
you got away with pretty much every change to his
house but being married to someone just because it
suits someone else is not me. I've done that Susie.
No chance. No thank you, but cheers all the same
for thinking about me'.
Jonathan and I continued to out-stare each other
with the ferociousness of six-year-olds in a
playground sandpit while one of Susie's many ex-
lover's, or whoever he was,

coughed for more attention, or maybe just to remove some more dirt particles, who knows, and said: 'There is, of course, something else which may or may not be upheld, but nevertheless I shall read now.'

And with a flourish more suited to that wonderfully fussy little Belgian detective, him with the perfect moustaches, Samuel Hillary blew away the remains of the dust from his papers, possibly back into the faded and lumpy rose-gold *damask*-covered chair which by now I had realised was for show only, and the solicitor delicately announced:

'Jonathan my love, Holly my dear sweet little friend, I loved you both so very much; you were my soul mates. I felt that you were each and all sides of me, the me I wanted to be. You represented the good in the world, the balance and the kindness I really wanted to deserve.

'I kept so much from you, but all I want now is for you both to be happy with each other. Happiness means trust. You must trust each other; you must tell each other the fondest memories of me, your funniest and maddest memories of me.

'Get to know each other, fall in love, and this time next year please be married. The lies I wove; I wove them to hide my greatest guilt.

'You both know something about me, and I know some things about you that would destroy our memories of each other.

'Isn't it better that you remember me with love and not hate, for all of our sake'.

Susie appeared to have taken unusually special care with the wording of the warning, but I had absolutely no idea which one particular incident could damage Jonathan.

And while he was looking at me, I could virtually visualise all the Susie conversations running through his head, perhaps trying to establish what was true and what had been foreplay teasing. I thought I saw a fleeting memory drifting through his subconscious and pausing as a caution on his perfectly symmetrical face.

And all the time, whilst still acting as the victorious sandpit bully, I was watching for any reaction from him and asking myself, did she not know me better? I moved away from either man's direct sight and sat down once more.

I have kept all of her stories right where they should be. Hidden and locked away. After all, some may have included my part in them, and I would never, ever tell him.

As much as I don't like him, she had a life before him – we all have. He deserves more than that. But what did she have about me?

*

And at that very same time Jonathan was thinking 'I wonder what she told me about Holly that can't be repeated?'

RECONSTRUCTING THE NORTHERN DAN

Dan Ingle was born in the Autumn of the 1960s in a cold and small rural cottage in a hamlet far enough away from Castleford, West Yorkshire, to be isolated in its own right, but close enough by to be classed as a pit-village, when it suited the *Union* men.

His father, Percy, had spent most of his working life after returning from the war, underground, and he brought the sadness of his long daily grind with him every evening.

On Fridays, after collecting his weekly pay-packet, he would meet for some beers with his working colleagues in the protective snug of *The Yorkshire Miner*. No bloody nagging women allowed in there, thank goodness; just good, proper dark ale you could almost chew on, and too many cigarettes. Afterwards he would return to his home motivated just enough to face his disappointing life until Monday came around again.

Dan's mother had passed her eleven-plus exam (with merit) to attend a good, solid, local and rather revolutionary Grammar School where the male teachers taught the girls, and the female teachers taught the boys. This methodology was revised after some close friendships resulted in marriages arranged in haste. Or worse.

Phylis Ingle excelled at her varied subjects and had the chance to stay on with her studies, but any future dreams would have coerced or beaten out of her by the financial demands of people who had her best interests at heart, if there hadn't been one of those hasty marriages at an almost legal age to Percy.

She thought that she had convinced him that babies born two months early can indeed be eight pounds and three ounces. With a tooth.

She now spent most of her married life removing the coal dust, grime, sadness and deeply ingrained Thatcher-filth from her family and her home, never appreciated or appreciating, but that was the way it was in those days in the biased North. Phylis also enjoyed her own choice of escapism, a tipple, a sweet sherry in a nice glass, on a Friday night, most nights actually, to numb her from the future she never would have chosen.

Dan knew he was expected to love his mother and bore the brunt of trying hard to express these false emotions towards her from both parents. He thought that his mother feared his father (finding out) more than she loved her son, if indeed any love remained, for this wasn't a family unit that was built on anything other than practicalities.

He also knew that joining his dad and many uncles working down the mine wasn't for him, the school nickname *Sissy* would probably have travelled down to the pit and the relentless dark humour along with it, and he wouldn't survive that.

Instead, he took the opportunity, whilst on a school day trip to York, by visiting the Army Careers office and signing up the very same afternoon.

Before and during his transition to become Daniella, and after he had left the Military, Daniel was a physical instructor for elderly people who needed to stretch out their ailments and complain about everything.

They expected a sympathetic ear, or at the very least, the appearance of a sympathetic ear, as most old complaining people don't really want to have a two-way conversation with a stranger, it's all about them, and as they were getting this service free of charge from the local GPs, they didn't really value the excellent work that Dan put in.

The GPs themselves were not hitting the targets set by the departments for trying to ensure the catchment list of their five thousand registered patients (for a three-man Surgery) were not only seen within an accepted timeframe, within a certain number of working hours in a restricted working week, to be given their ten minute slot, including the writing up of the notes, using the codes of time-wasters, repeat offenders and genuine ill health, to be included in the figures sent back to the government to give further support to destroy the National Health Service.

Because the elderly just wanted to talk. Forget any real ailments or heart-breaking loneliness, targets have to be hit and they can be hit, and the government figures fudged, when the old people are packed off with either a prescription for a placebo or a referral to Dan Ingle, physical instructor.

Before all of that, Dan was encouraged out of his Squadron after being caught with the Sergeant's wife's Sunday-best clothing on.

The Sergeant thought his wife had been unfaithful to him, she had, but not with Dan.

And so the non-commissioned officer ensured that Dan was manoeuvred out of his regiment, before their last tour of Iraq, and into the global *Military Intelligence Alliance,* unfortunately sharing the abbreviation with another military department, a network of the G20, part of the fortunate and privileged West. Upon his colleague's arrival in Basra, his former buddies were met with a mixture of roadside bombs and friendly fire from the Americans, as the ground intelligence received had most probably been fudged by the same underfunded government agency, monitored by untrained temporary staff, who collated every departments' figures.

The soldiers who came home in body bags were considered the lucky ones.

When Dan finally moved away from the Army and his roots in the grim North, where bias wasn't so dumb, he set up *CP Fitness,* in the more accepting Midlands. No-one knew him there, so he could make a fresh start. This movement and gentle exercise club was provided for the mis-understood and money-aware elderly. Named in part after his mother, Phylis. Sad, complaining Phylis, who he ultimately had realised was always going to be bitter and twisted, as when she could have made some changes she had opted not to.

CP Fitness, for the other complaining pensioners, was open seven days a week, and this was where Dan developed his first real crush. On Holly.

Holly had taken her mother along for the free coffee, black, no biscuits, as her mother, being a functioning anorexic, allowed herself a treat now and then, perhaps annually, and only after the exhausted local general practitioner, realising that the pill coatings may have calories so wouldn't be taken, had suggested that some movement of the limbs would help the blood flow to her cold heart. The doctor hadn't actually said out loud, what he had said was that this would help with the blood flow to her cold hands and feet. Much better than some suitable and scientifically researched tablet.

But that would have been an on-going extra cost for the NHS and lead to the GP being forced to take on more patients to balance the fudged figures.

Holly had told Dan that she 'cooked the books for a variety of businesses', which magnificently understated her actual business aptitude, but caring for her mother who didn't live with her and her two children that did, following a not-so-recent divorce where she still hadn't seen any regular monies in five years of fighting, other than the mandatory child support, had led her down this path of self-employment and as a result being available to everyone at any time.

Except to her best friend.

Holly said she would happily sort out his accounts, get the VAT returns returned monthly, establish if not a five-year cash-flow forecast then definitely a twelve-month one, and generally ensure the NHS paid for his valuable service within their typical 90 days payment structure, simply by invoicing on time. During this period, and over the next few months that followed, she spent a lot of time listening to Dan's stories, running his fitness centre when he flew (many times) to Thailand, where *Kathoeys* are acknowledged as a fully integrated sector of society.

After his full acceptance of himself and his desire to live his life as the woman he was, she joined him on his long and painful journey, encouraged him to start the transitioning by the hormone treatment on the NHS (later than usual but still recommended), attending so many consultations with the objective and supportive plastic surgeons, and ferociously fighting his corner whenever it was needed.

Holly helped with filling in all of the paperwork, countless and contradictory forms, and took him to the numerous psychometric assessments, as well as dealing with all of the pushbacks, the tears and any misplaced doubts, which were many.

Holly held his lovely warm and strong hands during the despair and the wobbles, and she was there when people at his fitness group, mostly the younger relatives, gawped at his newly painted nails and when he first started to wear more suitable, appropriately stunning and feminine clothes.

The elderly thought of him as a bit of a treat and loved him regardless.

Holly was waiting for him in the private ward when they shaved his Adam's apple, and later took her to *M&S* for her first, proper, bra-fitting. Something that Holly had never bothered with herself.

Now Daniella, six foot one inches of pure womanly gorgeousness, with the despairing legacy of the coal dust still deep in her soul and the scars of early life with clumsily covered army tattoos (later lasered perfectly), was to return all of this support, and for Holly, she would have given up her life.

Daniella Ingle, it would appear, was most definitely the perfect man for the job in hand.

THE FAMILY THERAPIST AND SUSIE

Dr Harriet Palmer, Dr Harry to her regulars, now
dwindling but by her own design, she reminded
herself often, was once again fighting a losing battle
with the pounding hangover from last night's lonely
drinking. She was relieved to see that today's first
session was with Mrs B (not always code-named as
Mrs B as she had been seeing Harriet for a long
time, and well before she became Mrs B, but a
recent addition of a very efficient personal assistant,
her mother-in-law as a trade-off for living with
Harriet rent-free, since she had given up all of her
cleaning duties, was determined to revamp and
update the patient files, for 'confidentiality purposes'
hence Dr Harry's clients sounding as though they
were auditioning for a *Quentin Tarantino* film). Mrs B
was Susie.
As Susie typically did most of the talking and the
direction of the sessions, Dr Harry could maintain
the safe facade of nodding. She occasionally offered
a random word or a grunt of comfort and some
encouragement whilst documenting the repeated
phrases (patterns in speech led to better
understanding and separating truth, and for Susie to
hone those repeated duplicitous wishes).
Trying to satisfy her thirst she drank lots of room-
temperature *Adam's Ale* (as her Gambian mother-in-
law called it, who herself once had a dream of
marriage with an already married and very young
Insular Celt-speaking stockbroker, which had
resulted in the unwanted Manlafi.

77

She was left with a huge bump, two hundred
Scottish pounds, and no more knee-tremblers over
his hard desk when he ran away to yet another
financial capital; leaving Kaddy, and his legal wife,
behind).

Harriet drank water, left overnight in the metal jugful,
by the jugful, in the hope of rehydrating herself,
getting the right amount of sodium into her brain
without overdosing with the fluid part. Trying to stop
her hands from shaking as they had taken to doing
as a result of the constant twenty-four-hour excess
and withdrawal cycle of alcohol. Rinse and repeat.
The moisture had the anticipated side-benefit of
allowing the English language to restructure once
again. To find form on her tongue. Hence the grunts
until that point.

Water that has been left to stand remembers its
purpose. By the time the water has run through old
pipes and lead taps and the many bends, it has
totally forgotten its meaning.

She recalled a young Indian female police officer
saying that to her some years ago. This was around
the time when she finally accepted that something
was not quite right with her husband.

Maybe that was the real reason Harriet had given up
being a GP. Water has a memory. Wine destroys it.
Dr Harry didn't need those memories of her
husband.

And Dr Harry, a person who lived within the shadow
of her own self-realised memories, and as a result of
this she lived in constant distress, needed any type
of anchor when facing Susie's fabrications.

Today Mrs B, robed in a sheath of a dress, carmine red, and as usual one size too small to showcase her fabulous assets, her décolletage was starting to crease and was a tiny bit bouncy now, perhaps due to excess sunbathing and the wrong types of supporting bra, but still worth watching nonetheless, with her matching shoes and always, always a fake designer bag, told Dr Harry her latest joke: 'I told my therapist I was hearing voices, he said I don't have a therapist!'

Susie had wanted to discuss her daughter, Abigail, when aged thirteen and finding herself up the duff. And Susie wanted confirmation that having the abortion had been the right thing to do. For herself, for Abigail and for women in general, after all, it was their lives, right? And again, it's our bodies, it's mostly always the woman's responsibility to bring them up, feed them, guide them.

Typically, Susie hadn't addressed the other issue, that of the child being seriously underage.

And neither had the therapist, as she may have exposed her own knowledge and experiences with the father of the foetus.

Susie said something about why would anyone really want to bring children into the world where they wouldn't get to know their real fathers. As if mothers don't count enough as a single parent.

And whilst Susie liked to float around on the cusp of feminism, she thought it could potentially put suitable lovers off, as she wasn't too sure of what it entailed. It took her best friend to brutally explain that if she put her hand down her knickers and found a fanny then she was a feminist.

'You're a fucking woman, Susie you deluded moron' Holly had said kindly. 'By default you're a feminist.' Susie had once picked up a Caitlin Moran novel by accident and read the back cover blurb to expand her mind, nearly buying it, but had seen enough by then and so picked up a sudoku quiz book instead. She had listened to plenty of talk radio and inane (male, of course) television presenters taking the piss out of feminists, so she knew for certain they were all lesbians, and she thought she knew enough about words such as 'objectify' and 'safe space' to sprinkle into her tales and fill out her well-informed anecdotes. The irony of that was what drove Holly mad. Deluded, she had said, more than once.

The therapist knew that abortion ran in Susie's nuclear family, and if the pun itself didn't amuse her, (the grunting in the right places helped both of them) watching her client trip herself up over the lies she had previously shared in earlier sessions almost certainly did.

Sometimes Susie's rationales for her own abortions were for the right reasons. In the Gospel according to Susie that was, rewritten many times, much like the other Gospels, it might be said. For instance, she didn't have enough love for another child, she certainly didn't care that much for her own. Or this truthful one, always an id-defending reason, she had needed a new car and a new marble work-surface for her latest kitchen renovation. All of this confusion certainly gave Susie plenty of scope for losing herself in her own inventive narrative – and it wasn't even a very good or particularly engrossing yarn to start with.

If we are to weave our own lies about our past, surely, we would make this into something worth remembering.

Better yet, as one of Harriet's favourite authors Mark Twain had said: 'If you tell the truth you don't have to remember anything'. In Susie's defence she always tells the truth. Even when she's lying.

With Susie, although she would tell anyone pretty much anything, she spun her own web of so many lies around her seemingly intense and pretty fragile ego. Those lies became her best versions of herself, her own sense of who she really was. And like most software upgrades, she lost the old flaws and stored memories.

Except they weren't lost, just filed away to resurface at low moments, to trip her back into her guilt, the one place she couldn't escape.

Susie inherited other people's stories that became her own. Like the time she didn't have dengue fever when she met the Cambodian survivors, or the time she did some undercover work for an ex-friend who was then married to her second husband. Or the time that she discovered her new husband had a sister, and his niece had been murdered in horrible circumstances.

Separating the wheat from the chaff and the lies from the truth was not for this therapist. Dr Harry's job was to simply listen, and let Susie work it out. Any other professional therapist would have been horrified at this approach, but it worked.

For all interested parties it seemed.

SUSIE'S SURVIVORS

Susie's two non-aborted children developed in the most unique of ways. The lovely strawberry-blond-haired little boy hummed and rocked steadily to his food, perhaps a mindfulness meditation in accepting some sort of kindness from the motion, whereas the daughter dressed up in her mother's clothing and experimented with smudged-black eye make-up and provocative underwear from the age of six, and had stopped eating when she hit her teens.

I had written to all of the major supermarkets with regards to the sexualisation of our children with my question of 'is this acceptable', but their lawyers had a better way of twisting my words, and the response was not only patronising, apparently that range was the biggest seller, the little ladies loved it, but they also took the time to kindly thank me for bringing this to their attention. And they included a voucher for my concerns. I bought wine.

Abigail was my main worry. Such a beautiful and bright girl who watched a different man leave her mum's bedroom every alternate Saturday morning (the one in between was when she couldn't get a babysitter and that was, on occasion, my big night out round at theirs). Her hair was so unbelievably black and in total contrast to Susie's natural fairness. Her clear hazel eyes also belonged to someone other than her mother, certainly not her father.

She truly was a stunning stick-insect of a child. And, maybe because of this, Susie was very cruel to her. Depending on her mood she would call her Abby, if she was good, and Gail if she wanted to hurt her. Pretty mean coming from a Susan.

As a result of the lack of consistent loving, of any type of loving, Abigail found a kind of control with food, as she became even tinier her boobs got bigger, blessings from her mother.

And as Abby got desperate for affection of her own, she experimented with her own sexual partners from a very early age.

Looking back, I guess I could have stepped in and replaced the need for love and affection with a hug and some kind words of advice and solid Holly guidance, but I didn't.

Abby had her first abortion at thirteen. Susie's reaction was super laid-back *laissez faire*, which would have won her the parent of the year award in any other circumstance, but this didn't stop the next two clinical visits before her daughter reached fifteen.

Social Services tried to take Abby away after someone in her neighbourhood blabbed, not me for once.

At the same time they took a good long look at rocking-Tommy, but as their home was clean and nice, and in a very desirable area, and while the kids may have been thin you could see they were well nourished (they checked the fridge and freezers, plenty of food) they didn't take his situation on board. He wasn't the one who had been reported after all. Susie broke down beautifully when she told them how hard it is being a single parent and having to do so many jobs to keep a roof over their heads; and with this, the social workers drank their expensive, freshly ground organic coffees, patted her arm and left her to her own devices.

They too were target-driven and this particular close-knit family from a nice area meant that the report could be filed away quicker than others, another tick for the government statistics.

Tommy's self-esteem was always at rock bottom. In the awkwardly named *First Fluffy Feathers* class at infant school, fledglings still learning to fly, (for the children who hadn't mastered basic functions, those of tying shoelaces and going to the lavatory by themselves) and where Tommy still hummed and rocked to his food enduring the relentless teasing from the rest of the class, he maintained his lovely, remote and passionless humour. He hung around with the naughtiest five-year-olds all the way through junior school with their regular night-time detentions, and then watched them narrowly avoiding being detained at Her Majesty's Pleasure (although I have often wondered why the Queen would have taken any pleasure in this) for the extra-curricular scrapes they got themselves into. When he was older, the little blond gang were all expelled together from the only senior school that would take them. On the radar first for the drug taking and later being so obvious in the dealing. Was there a way of telling Susie that she may need to be more hands on?

'Susie, do you think Tommy needs a bit of fatherly guidance?' I once dared to ask.

She looked at me, quickly replacing the automatic though fleetingly defensive expression with her defensive-victim look.

'I'm only saying that because you're so busy' said Holly the coward, 'and he's such a lovely kid that maybe you shouldn't be trying to do this all by yourself.'

'His father is a sad and useless sack, only ever good for money' she had said as she turned away from me.

But I'd seen Andrew, husband number two, in action with those children and didn't agree. And so, with my usual bravado, I dropped the subject, yet again.

Later that same year, as I can recall, Susie and I took the children away to mainland Spain for two weeks. I packed a huge suitcase between the three of us, she had a case for evening gowns, stiletto's and condoms and another, smaller one, for her kids' swimming gear. How did I not know in advance the type of holiday she was hoping for?

We landed after midnight and I was left in charge of four very tired children, three suitcases, and a key with a map to our apartment, whilst she went off in search of the priorities. A bottle of wine, a corkscrew and lots of ice.

I didn't believe my best friend was knowingly selfish; I just thought she genuinely had no clue about other people and their emotions.

And who am I to judge. Who is anyone to judge another. We each tread our own paths and all of that. Maybe we ought not to follow all the self-help twaddle and actually reach out to each other.

Not that I did that either.

I think the Spanish holiday brought her tally of successes up to more than five sides of the A4 piece of paper we had been comparing notes with, and that was with rather small handwriting, not including the surnames even when known, but a reference to place, occasion or prowess. *Pencil-dick Pedro* was my favourite. Never felt a thing.

And yet I carried on watching my friend with awe and admiration for her get-back-up-again time-after-time determination, and we still drank the semi-horrible wine, and she still sobbed late at night.

The kind of weeping where you don't know how the pain started or how ingrained it was, but the legacy of it is enough to keep you battling in the past regardless of whether they were real or imaginary armies.

I guessed if the grass really wasn't getting any greener it certainly got easier for her to flatten.

THE THROWBACK THERAPIST AND HOLLY

Holly hadn't seen Dr Harry since the funeral.
She didn't really mind that she had cried in front of
her, or that she was £75 lighter as a result of it, small
change for such a magnificent hug, her longest
physical contact in as many years as she could
recall. She was never hugged as a child.
And so when Dr Harry greeted her at the literally
stained glass-door even before she had rung the
ancient bell, she felt she really had made
improvements, if only for a different reason
altogether.
Observing the over-stretched black trousers and
swaying hips of her therapist completely without
judgement, as was her way, Holly followed Harriet
down the scuffed *Minton* floor corridor complete with
the appropriately hand-woven and worn *Kilim* rug,
maybe once fabulous but now rather suspiciously
old lady or mad cat wee tainted with just about
perfect *Rorschach* butterfly stains.
The headache-triggering odour from the cheap air-
freshener didn't hide the smell coming from the rug,
which was still damp after the liberally recent
spraying. The aromas merging in an aromatic
explosion, and therefore probably hugely toxic too.
Scent of a fine nylon lavender. Hideous.
Holly admired the abstract art hanging haphazardly
on the hall walls as though she hadn't really noticed
them before.
A number of limited-edition silk prints of dogs and
cats, only the one hundred and fifty done in total,
allegedly, and before the talented artist had
accidentally gassed himself at his garret in Bradford.

Hopefully not from inhaling the same noxious chemicals that had greeted Holly today. The pictures may eventually be worth something. Holly was seeing extra colours in the frames that she hadn't paid much attention to in earlier visits. Quite possibly a side-effect from the fumes. She had so much to tell her therapist.

'Dr Harry', she said, chuckling, 'She's only gone and left me her kids!!' The thing about Holly is that she actually used to be such great fun. An infectious sense of humour that had been leaking away since experiencing the gas-lighting and water-boarding abuse from *Itch*. This was now bubbling to the surface again. A bit like that dam up in Whaley Bridge.

A genuine broad laugh lit up the whole of her face, her eyes sparkling and the pink gums around her not so perfect white teeth which were now on full display and drying up, so her top lip didn't come down for a while.

The predicament was that Dr Harry had joined many of the dots already. It had taken her some time, and so she already knew a version, but not the whole story, albeit far from her to have to say anything. But there's a gossip girl in all of us and as Harriet was once one of us, she needed to hear all of the missing details.

Holly didn't tend to alter the occasion to suit her own needs, unlike the other now-fading star in both of their constellations, she spoke with honesty and humour.

This would be fun and would perhaps do Holly good. So said the failed older woman to herself, her defensive id doing its level best to protect that even older ruined ego of hers.

Holly was guided to sit in a sad and obviously unloved living room. Not the usual treatment room with its faux yellow support.

A special honour in this never-before-visited personal space, as it would appear no misguided therapy would be relevant today, or any day onward, if truth was told.

This room being equally as out of date as the rest of the house, although all of the rooms she had ever seen had carried a sense of sadness, a great weight of failure, this one was a serious contender for group wrist slitting.

The fading speckled nylon carpet, once oatmeal, that ran through the majority of the house, harboured much dejection from histories past. The hot coal burns dating back before the common sense of putting a rug over them was ever suggested, and long before an electric fire was installed, something was needed to hide the failures of the melted fibres. And was that seriously wood-chip paper? Painted over and over many times with a traditional and uncompromising magnolia shade. Covering up so many unhappy observations.

An ancient printer sat forlorn and irrelevant next to a computer which had its USB cable attached, and an old video player was hooked up to the television.

Some boring therapist stuff to watch on the big screen, Holly surmised.

The limp, once blue, velvet curtains looked as though they would close themselves over the drooping yellowed nets out of pure shame and humiliation for being on such public display.

It was clear that jolly Kaddy's obsessive cleaning compulsions had not found their way into this terrible gloom.

The dust on last year's Christmas hyacinths covered up the overwatered and rotten bulbs. This was truly a horrible room and for a short time Holly wondered why she was here.

Susie would have loved this make-over challenge.

It was not a warm space, in spite of the latest appliance being cranked up to full blast, with the chance of melting more of the polyamide by the downward position of the fan.

Holly could feel both the damp from the vast open space and the sadness of Harriet's many sorrows seeping gloomily into her bones.

It certainly was not a room to encourage any deep confessions, so when the therapist's footsteps were heard coming back down the hall, Holly realised she wasn't inclined to share so much after all.

'Tell me everything' Dr Harry demanded as she returned with the mismatched teacups and saucers and an actual teapot cosy that she had found in the loft. This being one of the many trinkets her mother-in-law had appropriated from one of her London clients whilst being the *jolly black girl* – as a leaving present, she might have said.

Harriet blew away any evidence of Bill Haley from the woolly *lugger* and from the inside of the cups, plonking the tray down so heavily the stained teaspoons rattled, waiting to see if this was the beginning of the process where Holly would start to unravel the maliciousness of her dead best friend, all by herself.

'Oh, but before you spill, can I just show you something?' And with that, Harriet Palmer headed towards the TV.

AFTER THE LOVE HAS GONE

Jonathan had started to feel something. Although he couldn't quite isolate the emotion, he suspected it may have been a hurt of some kind. It could have been that he just missed all the lights on when he came home, although he didn't miss the huge electricity bill. He genuinely missed his dinner ready in the oven, when she had found the time to cook for him. He thought he missed calling her when he was on the way back home from his local office, and getting her to meet him in their favourite wine bar. He missed the shallowness of how he felt in the way people looked at him when he was with her. And he couldn't stop thinking about how he got her to marry him after such a short romance. He had actually thought it was his idea for a while. Such a fool.

He had a fleeting thought that he should phone Holly for advice. So he didn't.

Holly, in the meantime was doing her duty beyond anyone's call, taking Susie's sad offspring out to an early supper with her own younger children twice a week every week after the funeral. On these occasions she put her ethics to one side and rather than support a local and independent restaurant they went to a pub chain where you could guarantee the same microwaved food fare and fun decor, time after time.

Tommy was beyond entertaining. He was withdrawn and unsociable, not like his old self at all, most possibly due to the cannabis, judging from the skunk odour that emanated from his discoloured clothes.

His eyes were sore and red from crying; they were bloodshot from smoking, and his usual soft but smart-ass approach was gone, along with any sense of normality. Abby, on the other hand, had flourished and had taken over Susie's mantle. Every man is a possibility. She had strutted over to the table having come in a taxi from Jonathan's house, sashaying her fabulous figure for every male's attention. Holly said she reminded her of her mum, and this made Abby hang her head with the appearance of sadness, although her eyes were proud and without tears when she looked up again.

Holly asked them both how Jonathan was doing but neither offered a thing. She would have like to have put this down to their concern and long chats with him, but knew that the truth was neither of them had even considered his pain, or even really talked to him. They weren't the type of young adults who had learnt to comprehend another's suffering. Their mum had taught them well.

And so, Holly eventually caved in after this last meal and called Jonathan, as not only did they need to sort out Susie's children and their future home and schooling and the many financial implications involved here, they may also have to address the twelve-month project.

Holly and Jonathan met later that same week in a restaurant half-way between their respective homes. The reviews said it catered for every bad taste, and it didn't disappoint. Holly had the vegetarian special, which was mostly noodles and some bland over-steamed vegetables; just what is it with the obsession of water chestnuts?

93

Jonathan showed his true colours with total disregard for her beliefs, and ordered the mixed grill. Later, when he offered his steak knife for her to cut the cheese, she would have cheerfully slit his throat with it.

Holly was already thinking that this man was just horrible, when he had the audacity to choose the wine too.

She doesn't drink red like Susie did when Susie was with him. She had stained teeth as a result, that and the inner rim of her lips mixing with her BJ lipstick, but it didn't stop her teasing him, in full display of any other diners. Actually, that used to embarrass the hell out of him, if truth be told. That evening he chose a cheeky little French Merlot. Using her way of speaking too. Holly waited until the waiter poured his tasting wine before ordering her own glass of something, white and even more cheeky, judging by the price.

Holly considered asking him how he was doing but was waiting for him to ask her. After all, she had known Susie longer, she knew her a lot better. She knew things about her that would make him examine his wedding tackle with the *Hubble* telescope every morning and night for signs of alien life form – and she could make a best guess for defining the origin of each species. Shit. Would she tell him? If that's the best Holly has on Susie to be forced into this farce, then it really was the biggest joke ever.

And as time waits for no man, especially a dullard forensic footman, it became clear that he wasn't into small talk that evening, any time really, so Holly eventually asked him how he was doing.

He said he was fine. She asked him if he was lying and gave him that pink gummy smile to soften the harshness of her words, the one she usually gave to make people feel she actually cared.

Unfortunately for Holly he was suckered right in. Words fell from him, so many words, more than she had ever heard in all the time they had avoided each other.

He said he didn't know how to feel anything. He said how he missed the noise that surrounded Susie, (this was due to her one-ear deafness as a result of a severe beating by her stepfather and so every television in every room of his house was always on at full blast). He said he missed her meeting him at the wine-bar.

Holly asked him if he really missed the lift home and smiled that smile again. He carried on, so obviously falling into her managed kindness, and said but I don't miss her really. Early days perhaps, suggested the steady smile.

And so, while all this one-sided support was going on, Holly was waiting for Jonathan to ask her how she was doing, and she was thinking how she could have helped him to fit all these emotions together. That she could explain the grief process and the stages to look out for – those to congratulate yourself on when getting through them.

And then she could be concise and precise about how she felt about losing her dear, dear friend, but she thought 'you don't want to know do you?

'You don't see anything outside of your blinkered stupid life. God in your heaven, and hallowed be in whatever name, just what is it I am meant to be learning from this experience'.

When Jonathan finally noticed Holly was still sitting there and they had sat in silence for a very long time, he asked her how the children were. She said yours or mine and laughed her genuine laugh, out loud.

Jonathan had never heard Holly laugh before. It was always Susie that made the joke and Susie who had laughed at it first, she said that was because she knew the punchline. And Holly would accept Susie laughing as though that was all that really mattered.

All that really matters to Holly right now is to make it through the evening, ha, nearly said the night then, what a hideous thought.

She tells Jonathan that as much as it's important that they support each other through this horrible time, he really doesn't have to propose to her.

'Whatever dreadful secret we both may hold is nothing to what we feel for Susie and what terrible comeuppance could befall us if we simply did nothing?'

It's always interesting though, to watch another person try to think things through.

Either this man knows something monstrous, or he feels enough loyalty to his dead wife to go through with this daft scheme, or he has swallowed something the wrong way and the expression on his stupid, red podgy face is because he is trying not to retch.

Jonathan was doing his best to appear involved in the conversation but needed to get a glass of water. He didn't dare ask Holly as it was a piece of his medium to rare fillet steak that was stuck, and he knew she would let him choke.

So, she watched him suffer and chose to ignore the struggle for a while, and instead said: 'I think the dilemma is this, Susie did something dreadful that she never told me about. This either happened before she met me, in which case how can it affect me, or during our friendship, which must mean I'd know about it – she never could keep a secret. By me never finding out, is she protecting me from some hideous truth, but if it is so hideous, surely she couldn't protect me forever?'

Then finally she relented and pushed her last drop of bottled water over to Jonathan before he passed out. It really was not his fault he was such an idiot.

THE SAME AFTERMATH, BUT LATER

Holly was wondering what she knew about him that she is fearful of his finding out? He knows his wife flattened plenty of grass in her time, although nowhere near the exact numbers, because even Susie didn't know that. And so, it can't be the list of previous suitors. Susie may have been the world's biggest hypochondriac and she must have feared for her health with all those germs flying around, but Holly never heard that she had caught anything. Well, except crabs, and Susie thought this was an amusing story to tell everyone at any opportunity she had. *Sandy MacNabs* she called them. Though why she would be combing her lady garden no-one ever wanted to know.

Holly briefly wondered if she'd confided in her something that was really important and was it on one of those many occasions when she was tuning into every third word out of politeness and only then if it sounded remotely interesting.

Jonathan watched Holly that night. He thought he could see every thought, no matter how fleeting or for how long she held onto it. Her face, falling when she didn't realise anyone was looking, showed the pain and confusion that he felt he ought to have been feeling. But he still wasn't.

Maybe they both would have liked Susie to have pulled up a seat and play the evening back to them. She would have made Jonathan look a total idiot for ordering the wrong wine; she would have royally berated him for ordering meat, knowing that Holly abhorred all kind of animal abuse.

And she would have made the right kind of entrance – all eyes would have been on her. And maybe that's what Jonathan missed the most. Her drama.

When it was about time to say goodnight, Holly didn't want to be too obvious, so she said instead that the waiters have their pyjamas on and is that a hint.

For some reason, she was happy when she saw it annoyed the life out of him when she didn't just say it's time to go. She couldn't miss an opportunity to dress the brutality up, but didn't know why he, of all people, would bring this side out of her.

Jonathan suggested he drove her home and seemed affronted when she pointed to the empty bottle of red and wiggled her single glass of white at him.

Holly suggested they ought do it again but stopped short of telling him that it had been fun. He told her it was a real pleasure, and that they should think about their dilemma, which immediately changed the dynamics of the evening.

And she knew from his watching the expression on her face that he was reading her innermost thoughts: 'Who the fuck is this guy? God, here am I ready to feel sorry for him and he dares to think he can possibly have a smarter solution to all of this than me? What do they say about never arguing with an idiot?

'Bloody hell Jonathan' she said angrily and very loudly.

'What insane dilemma? Your wife, my best friend, cooked up the most idiotic idea about us getting married and then wants to throw a spanner in the works to ensure that we do?

'Well, I have plenty of stories to tell about her, but I won't ever pass them on. Ever. She loved you. End of.'

And now he is confused. And Holly is hoping he's thinking 'what stories?' but it doesn't look like he is. Jonathan watched her as the condescension fell from her face.

'I'm sorry' he said. And then he started to choke up again but this time it was real sorrow. When those teardrops fill your eyes and you don't have the energy to blink them away, as they roll one by one covering your face, each following the line of the others as though they can blur their final destination, and in doing so mask their origin. Travelling from a place so many times visited, deep shudders of abandonment. Made much worse as he simply didn't know why he was crying.

Holly just touched the back of his hand, because she understood, and knew he needed nothing further than this.

She called her local taxi driver to take him home and said to put the journey on her account.

He cried harder because this is something Susie wouldn't ever have thought of doing, and he simply don't know anything, anymore.

Under normal circumstances she may have driven him home. But the last thing she needs right now is someone making a clumsy pass at her because they wanted her to be somebody else. She'd done that once before.

'I'm sorry Jonathan. You'll never know how much.'

TAXI!

Jonathan always had his alarm pre-set to 6.30am
wherever he was in the world and didn't alter this on
that strange day, mainly because he had forgotten
to, but mostly because it had been his earlier
intention to enjoy a good long hike to repatriate his
car. He must have always known he was going to
drink too much, and therefore planned to walk the
anticipated hangover away.
He felt an excruciating emptiness when he woke up
alone, having woken more than once during the
night, and this, coupled with a new raw emotion, as
yet unidentified, overwhelming him to the point
where he really did feel something like shame taking
over him. His mind, body and soul ached.
Something very unusual was beginning to engulf
him. And with this simple exhaustion he realised he
just couldn't be bothered to walk to the car.
The alcohol abuse and last night's awkwardly
recalled embarrassing behaviour added to his newly
released sadness, mixing this up with a heavy dose
of the very basic lack of too much red-wine-induced-
energy. He had carried on with his lonely drinking
when he had got home.
Jonathan thought he would ask Tommy to give him a
lift, but, as was becoming his habit, Tommy had
enjoyed his own habitual late-night drinking session
with Jonathan's vodka, and massive weed-fest
(Jonathan really did need to speak with them both
again about some basic housekeeping rules, and to
address the practicalities of shipping them both back
to their father) and couldn't, or more than likely,
wouldn't, be woken.

After a hot shower, hot fresh towels, (laundered by
Abby as she didn't want to go back and live with her
father and his fussy wife), and plenty of black coffee,
he demolished the whole pot in half an hour,
Jonathan called the same taxi company that had
escorted him back the evening before. The business
card had been left on the shelf, along with his keys,
the number entered into his phone by the ever-
thoughtful Holly. Both of these had been abandoned
late last night through his continuing waterfall of
tears.
As luck would have it, it was the same fabulous
African driver, Chibuike, who came to collect him.
The night before he had chatted all the way back to
Jonathan's home, he told the podiatrist about his
own feet, everyone always does this, and so the
podiatrist assessed that he could indeed rob a bank
and not leave a footprint, which was just an attempt
at fun on Jonathan's part.
Chibuike was saying that when he first came over to
England to make his money he had fully intended to
go back as soon as his wife's mother would let him,
and open a fine rum bar on the beach. Then, if his
wife would let him, he would fill it full of the finest
cocktails and the prettiest girls and watch them
dance all night and then replace the dancing with the
sunrise and the calm of the blue and green waves
for the yoga people, all of the day round, share some
happiness.
To be honest, he said, his time in the Western world
had completely jaded him.

'How come when we all have so much, when we are so rich, do we do nothing but complain all the time? No wonder the sun always goes down so early in England, Mister Feet'.

Today Chibuike was saying if he had met a girl like mine (Holly?) then he wouldn't have been crying last night, no Mister Footman, I would hold her tight, and kiss her and tell her she is like the sweetest violet flower in the whole of that pretty English garden.

'Mate', Jonathan said awkwardly, 'I think that someone else once said violet delights, violence ends.'

And he looked away as they shared an awkward laugh, as only men, so completely out of touch with each other's reality, can.

THE CONSTANT GARDEN THERAPIST AND SUSIE

Harriet Palmer later recalled a particularly bright start to that specific morning. As she threw the curtains wide, she saw the sun was already high and requesting a precise salutation.

As a result of having recently discovered yet another *YouTube* Guru, she had taken to bowing to the original first element three times a day. No such thing as the first element, a more experienced text-book Yogi had said knowingly.

There was no sign of the newly deafened Bill Haley either, or his stinking mess in the utility room.

Her mother-in-law was still tucked up in bed and Harriet experienced a real *Schrödinger* cat moment of bliss. Only yesterday she had achieved practically 8000 steps. Well, just over 7000.

As things were certainly looking up, she rewarded herself with the remains of last night's take-out, dry spare-ribs, for breakfast. And some prawn crackers, washed down with diet Coke; as a gesture.

Mrs B arrived slightly late, as was her way, which didn't affect the billing.

Today she was dressed in yet another new outfit, a two-piece in white linen with rose splashes, too tight as always and far too short (Holly used to tell her to close her legs because of the draught).

Susie completed this look with a matching *Joan Miro* inspired rose-like primary school splashes, on yet another fake designer handbag. Holly had once told her that she dressed as per her many room makeovers.

Susie hadn't taken much offence, she probably thought it was a compliment.

She happily announced: 'I've done it Doctor Harriet! I've made a new Will, and where there's a Will there's going to be a new revelation!'

Dr Harry had already boiled the water for the coffee, which was freshly ground by the useful delicatessen yesterday, and whilst the milk was frothing, not microwaved, she brought the tray over to the table along with the yellow milk jug and white spotted yellow coffee cups, no saucers for coffee said some etiquette guru.

Early on in her self-made transition from practitioner to therapist she had attended many online and off-the-wall holistic courses; initially to dispel alternative treatments.

She was sceptically surprised and delighted to find some of these had real results. One of them had been the introduction of certain therapeutic colours. Yellow, it would appear, is a bit of a secret weapon. Although terribly overused these days, said the etiquette guide.

Another secret weapon, one that ought to be used more often in general, is that of listening without thinking about making any response.

Dr Harry took her creamy, sugary coffee back to her high-backed chair, the yellow scattered cushions with genuine, not shabby-chic frayed edges around the zip, due mostly to Bill Haley and his constant quest to destroy everything around and about her in his mission to hear again. Two cushions were needed to support the curvature of her spine.

She waited for Susie to jump into the gap.

Out of the consultation room's big wooden framed French windows, she saw that the sun had rewarded her earlier salutation and was shining directly onto the patio.

Dr Harry lost herself momentarily in the quiet and was focussed on the range of hand-painted clay pots, full of herbs she had long ago placed around the perimeter of the decking. The lemon grass was for deterring cats, the three types of lavender for the same purpose.

Holly had brought the lavender to encourage the bee population. The original planting pot with the fragrant peppermint, to deter any flies, needed watering, in fact the pot was far too small, but the last time she had tried to transplant any mint it had died. A typical reaction, she had later read. Mint will not be transplanted.

She was wondering about roots and disturbance, and whether the real reason people are constantly in pursuit of happiness is because of the original planting space, the womb, and therefore the sense of abandonment after birth, when she heard Susie say:

'I've been thinking about being dead.' Dr Harry knew best to let her continue, and as she wanted to explore the warm womb theory, all that was needed was a slight head tilt to imply she was still listening.

'Not that I'm planning it but if I die, and the children need a blood transfusion or a kidney what would they do, would they know to look within, or would they have to rely on anonymous donors?'

And with that Susie hugged herself and shuddered, dramatically.

Dr Harry turned her thoughts away from Thich Nhat Hanh. She had been treating Susie long enough to know what was behind this question, but, as with all good therapists, and those that refreshed their knowledge from magazines and many online gurus, she knew that the words and solutions needed to come from the client. She could only push the occasional dialogue and so she waited.

Susie may have appeared as though she actually wanted Dr Harry to tell her exactly how to act, and managed to keep silent for a few moments only, for her then to say:

'I've made a Will, Doc, stashed with my Law Society enemies, and with some pretty big hints in so that if I die someone can work it out, and then they will understand me and perhaps they'll eventually feel sorry for me.'

Some things will never change.

WHEN JONATHAN MET SUSIE

Jonathan met Susie on a Friday night at a popular nightclub outside the county town of Warwick.
He had just returned from a flight from the USA, certainly not the cheapest of airlines, first class too as the American authorities deemed him pivotal to them and therefore certainly worthy of Uncle Sam's IRS recently recovered monies, from their citizens, and partners, who had moved elsewhere in the world. Apparently they still had to pay US taxes. Thank you so much Mr Obama, Jonathan thought. So they had bumped him up, onto an airline that employed the older has-beens, as they were grateful for any job, and those weary staff who had been long passed over for younger and prettier staff were past caring if they poured the tepid and too-strong coffee over your hand and sleeve, knowing they couldn't be sued as individuals anymore, with a standard retort to anything being a sarcastic 'sorry sir / ma'am'.
He was bedraggled, confused, coffee stained and quite exhausted, which admittedly was usual for him, apart from the coffee, and he desperately needed to get home to assimilate the whole trip.
Jonathan had already committed to celebrating a friend's birthday before he went Stateside and couldn't now get out of the plan.
For one thing his UK mobile phone was still with the little despots in Customs, as he had unwillingly 'left' that with them before his flight out.
Although perhaps more accurately it was because the friend whose birthday it was on that day, had picked him up from the airport.

As a result, Jonathan was now propped up against the bar and with the help of jet lag, he was seeing double.

This trip had been more exhausting that his previous visits. The conferences and one-to-ones working with the world's best within the fidelity, bravery and integrity set-up, was followed by an investigation into an unsolved but fairly recent murder of a six-year-old girl. Twenty-five percent of all the bones in our framework are in one wonderfully complex human foot, but still this magnificent support is viewed by the public and doctors as an insignificant body part, only really noticed when something goes wrong.

The importance of foot shadows has long been overlooked, as Jonathan had made clear all of those years ago, but as footwear evidence is becoming more commonly understood in forensic situations, so has the pedal evidence. The feet and the footprint left behind, in a nutshell. And all they had to get their man for this murder, was a matching footprint. Jonathan had been in the state of Washington for a long eleven days, with just one of those days reserved at what the feds thought was the crime scene. The rest of the time there, with the exception of the actual conference, he had spent his hours immersed with the photographic evidence of the footprints, identifying the bare footprint with other footwear recovered from the perpetrator's trailer park house. Although there was only the one body and the one suspect, it was still important to plough through the podiatry records, just in case the smart lawyers further down the line found a chink in his analysis.

And when Jonathan was able to produce something that would be useful for the medical and criminal justice students, as well as for the podiatrists, the criminalists, any footwear examiners and forensic anthropologists, and obviously the people who would find the murderer guilty, everyone would be satisfied. A no-brainer.

The actual crime scene was in his six-year-old niece's bedroom. Up until the DNA exclusion tests, Jonathan wasn't aware he even had any siblings, let alone a niece. And maybe this was why he worked every minute that was left on that trip. Extending his stay for longer, he had to ensure the ends justified his means. Because as everyone knows, it is more common than not that the murderer is someone known to the family.

Memento Mori, remember you will die, he had thought.

And back to the here and now, with the fabulous floating from jet lag enhanced by some rather elegant New World Merlot with the pre-party meat feast, he could see Susie was a true vision.

Well, in truth, both Susie's were. With her cascading blonde hair and sexy hour-glass figure lighting up the room, she was smiling, laughing loudly, radiating energy and confidence. And she was looking directly at him. Jonathan took another swig of the marvellous French brandy.

He had little recollection of talking to her friend, although when meeting her sober a few months later he may have recalled the competition between them both for his attention (and he still doesn't know why).

He had gladly lost all of the memories of that night altogether, thank you guilt and alcohol, and so he had inherited Susie's creative version of events instead.

He genuinely didn't really know what happened. He knew he hadn't woken up with her the next day, and so when he found a telephone number written on his hand, he thought it best to write it out somewhere safe. And then he promptly lost it. Jonathan's everyday life, dull to some perhaps, but of a certain and safe regular routine to himself, carried on as normal. He filed the divorce papers with heavy sadness, and had his mobile phone returned from the customs people, where the call he had expected (and desperately needed) hadn't been received.

He considered approaching his mother, alone, about her daughter, but to introduce the idea of a grand-child when that child was now dead caused many sleepless nights.

The right thing to do versus the wrong thing to do. A dilemma a loving son shouldn't have to face, and an outcome that presented too many sad endings. Firstly, his mother may not have told his father about the baby, so for her to show any emotion would then have to be explained and may possibly undermine everything the two of them had gone through.

To not tell her could be equally as cruel, maybe she really did want to know what had happened to her little girl. In the end, he decided not to say anything for now.

Maybe when he was sorted from the divorce and things got back to whatever his new normal could be, he would take his parents to America and arrange for his mum to meet her abandoned daughter. Subject to them both agreeing to this of course.

So Jonathan carried on much as he ever did, in the familiar way he took comfort from. He came home from work either via the pub and his parent's house for tea, or the pub and some form of takeaway for the best part of every week. Then at the weekends he could lose himself in his recovery and would go fishing or shooting dependent on the season and depending on whether he needed silence or noise.

Some time went by in much the same way as it had for the previous fifteen years when he got a call from one of the lads who had been seconded to him from the police station, with a message that had been forwarded from the forensic pathology lab.

Apparently, some bird was after his number, but he took hers instead, for security reasons obviously, and did he mind if he pretended to be Jonathan for a chance of a leg-over?

Jonathan waited another few days before he called Susie. This wasn't due to any lack of confidence, after all, she had tracked him down.

It was more to do with the thought of yet another relationship so soon after his failed marriage.

Another effort of getting to know someone, their music tastes, their ambitions, their family, their way of life, the bathroom habits. Their histories, for goodness sake.

And to be honest, he was still so wrapped up in his own deceit, and the emotion and fear of the aftermath of his actions should they be uncovered, was he really ready for some more of his time to be invested in another failure?

Having rationalised all of that he did remember this was a very sexy and stunning woman. What harm would it really be? A lot of fun, some action obviously, and nothing more, he reasoned, back then.

Susie was delighted and shocked and surprised to hear from him and how fortuitous it was that he found her number after all this time. After all this time, yes. He couldn't tell her the real story, so he asked her out for a drink instead. Later it transpired that she knew quite a lot of the people at his workplaces and may have dated a couple.

She was such great company. So many hilarious and laugh out loud stories. A really alluring woman in all senses. Whenever they would walk into a pub or restaurant together everyone would turn to look at her, gawp, look at Jonathan and gawp some more. She immediately made friends with his friends and their strange village wives (interbred, she would tell Holly a long time later) and made everyone feel really welcome at his place, which she had skilfully begun to reconstruct.

Susie arranged barbecues for his work colleagues (those she hadn't slept with) marinating the kebabs and chops with her own blends and mixtures, purchased from her trusty Deli, so in effect she could claim them as her own.

She cooked fabulous romantic dinners at his lovely old cottage for just the two of them, while still running her successful catering business, and before he knew it, she had moved in and was arranging his next marriage.

During all of this beautiful and manipulative foreplay it meant leaving her children either on their own and to their own devices, or in the hands of this curious Holly, who he still hadn't been introduced to, although admittedly he had heard plenty enough about her.

And if he was going to be really honest, right at the beginning it hadn't occurred to him to ask who was looking after her children. He didn't care. She was with him. She had totally taken over his life, taken his mind away from America, from his recent divorce, from his guilt and his grief.

This was a real whirlwind romance and she lit up his life like she lit up other people's lives. Why would he want to judge this lovely woman, she made him feel a little less complicit, and for a short while he could just lose himself in her loveliness.

THE RELATIONSHIP THERAPIST AND HOLLY

Holly's last visit to Dr Harry had been the one where, for some strange reason, she had been treated to a home video of the marriage between her therapist and Manny Sarr. Something she certainly had little desire to see again. Holly had recognised her own husband and his regular plus one in many of the background shots. Rather than acknowledge this she just told Harriet that she looked 'a real cool cougar' and 'what a vintage frock!'

Holly was giving some serious thought as to how she could break her bond with this devious woman. Being generally passive-aggressive, she thought she could just wean herself away by giving this dreadful lady yet another chance at being of any use to her at all. At the same time, Holly could see if she had anything else she wanted to 'hint' at. Holly didn't know why she behaved in this way, she always had, but as she no longer relied on Susie for guidance, where she would always do the exact opposite, she instead determined that this session would be her last. Or one of the lasts. More dilly-dallying behaviours inherited from her dad. Can't upset anybody Holly, he would say.

Holly had brought another home-made cake, this time double chocolate with fresh cream, and yet another perfectly potted container of mint (as she'd noticed Dr Harry's last unsuccessful attempt at gardening). She had opted for Apple mint as it is also known as Woolly mint and that made her laugh out loud in the local pound shop. Holly also had some inexpensive cat snacks for Bill Haley which jiggled and rattled around his special little bag.

The cat purred and fussed and patted the red velvet pouch often (we really don't know who was being conditioned here) and even allowed Holly to tickle his ears as he rewarded her with a huge leap onto her little lap to snuggle down, causing some hot coffee to spill onto her leg, which certainly smarted a little. Cats, it would appear, do what the fuck they want.

Dr Harry pushed the mandatory box of cheap tissues over to Mrs H, a gesture only as the older woman didn't have children. Her husband once threw up after sex very early on in their marriage – they hadn't attempted anything during the courting rituals, as Manlafi Sarr had firmly told her that according to his culture, sex before marriage wasn't permitted, and so was this was never initiated again. And as a result of not being allowed to care, for husband or child, or indeed, herself, Harriet didn't know the importance of washing a coffee stain out straight away.

She would not know, as in Holly's motherly experiences, the importance of spit on a hanky for a dirty face and cream cleanser on the knees daily as bath time was once a week, usually Sunday, whether you needed one or not.

Some would say that in order to advise and guide people, it can't all be learned from a text-book. Life experiences are also required. Some others would just say to put some fancier tissues out, yellow maybe, to confuse everyone with appearances and all that crap.

Normal people wouldn't have kept a cat.

Dr Harry had read enough, and in her opinion, which she never shared with anyone as psychotherapists don't expose their own most inner thoughts, everything has a solution. Whether that is an extra dose of washing powder or a cat that needed to be euthanised with bare electricity wires attached to the non-green section of the National Grid. Much more powerful. Tell that to the animal-loving-Eco-Warriors. Harriet helped herself to a very generous portion of the wonderfully sticky cake, just under half, that had been made with milky warm liquid cocoa not powder. Holly's lovely, kind, paternal-nana shared that secret with her, amongst others, and as the greedy therapist sat back with a reassuring 'aaah' in her usual maddening manner, propped up by the two retro yellow cushions, she asked Holly how her mother was.

Completely out of the blue one may think, but Dr Palmer suspected Holly may be trying to cut some ties and so she needed to get back on track with some notion of therapy and not just enjoying the easy social time. She may also need the extra money just in case Manlafi came in hard. That would make a nice change, she thought.

Having a haphazard approach to her own life she perceived that all of us, at some time, experience 'new recognisable patterns of behaviour' from our parents, and so the mum question was always a 'go-to' safety net. If Harriet Palmer wasn't so reliant on her own coping mechanism, this being the over abuse of alcohol, and food, she may have actually made a half-useful counsellor.

'My mum?' Holly asked, with obvious surprise in her voice. 'Yeah, she's still breathing and blaming me for dad, critical of my life choices, the usual, but she likes the fact that I'm more available to her now, you know, after all this.' Her voice trailed off with the realisation that 'all of this' meant the death of her best friend, the draining emotions of her long and drawn-out divorce and the continuing money battles. Maybe even her mixed reaction to Jonathan.

'Can I talk to you about Jonathan instead' Holly asked, and to buy herself time and mask her own true feelings, she too reached for what was left of the sticky cake, but, as usual, never eating it.

Her actions showing another prop in our many armouries which deflect from our limited language, and the way we use words, into a positive action.

Uninvited, Holly talked about Jonathan. From the notes Dr Harry read later, it would appear that Holly didn't think Susie's children were totally happy there at all, but their own father had made no effort to collect them, which was weird wasn't it? She didn't think Jonathan was coping very well and do you think someone ought to talk to him? But perhaps more tellingly, she was showing some signs of real attachment to him, and for Holly, she did not need to have another relationship with someone who did not see her for what she really was.

Which was Dr Harry's humble, selfish, subjective, conceited and not thought-out-opinion. Totally inaccurate as well.

MISS MATCHES

Jonathan had inherited a very one-sided view of
Holly. If Susie and he had ever fallen out, which had
become more frequent of late (Susie managed his
every mood and the making up afterwards) it was
mostly because of Holly.

Susie constantly seemed to need to be in touch with
her. To know what she was doing and who she may
be doing it with. Nothing and no-one, usually, was
the answer. Susie had to be in daily contact. It was
always that way round. Holly would normally always
take her call and four times out of the ten invitations
they would get together, although if he remembered
anything at all now, it would be that Holly very rarely
called his wife and would often let Susie down at the
last minute. However, that didn't stop the Holly
conversation.

'She deserves the best from me' Susie had once
said, and when Jonathan made the silly man
mistake of asking the age-old and unanswerable
question of: 'Why?' he got something along the
following lines: 'No-one knows her like me. She is
everything I wanted to be. So sweet and kind. See
what a good friend she is, always baking stuff and
being there for everyone.' And, in fairness, he really
had tried hard to look.

The only thing he could see was a sharp and
sarcastic, tough and brittle, condescending woman,
who constantly disappointed his new wife.

Which was exactly what Susie needed to hear.

Holly, it would appear from Susie's many creative recollections, grew up as an afterthought, a single child to terribly ancient parents in a good old regular happy family.

Her mum was always at home, even though they really did need a second income as they were always so hard up, her parents had taken the view that you shouldn't have children if you weren't going to look after them yourselves. Her dad was the threat to keep her in check, although she was an easy-going child having watched out for the eggshells her father used to tease her he trod on around her mum. And she had ballet and piano lessons in the early days before that stopped being fun too. No-one went to watch the performances as her dad would have been working away and her mother did not hide her disinterest. Holly had told Susie she vaguely recalled winning a junior school scholarship for violin lessons but being made to practise in the cold garage meant she soon fell out of favour with that as well. You can't pluck strings with cold fingers, she said, which had Susie falling about.

Holly ploughed through school as only an un-impressed only-child could. Falling out with the teachers by asking questions away from the set curriculum, her fast brain meant she was genuinely interested in anything away from the time-tables. She didn't fit in with the in-crowd, although she admired them hugely from a distance.

Never really achieving anything in the formal educational-scoring-stakes but knowing she was safe and loved was more than enough, her dad often told her.

Although really, she didn't know how safe and loved was interpreted until she was a lot older, but by then any damage was done and the opportunity to blame her parents was long gone.

Holly's mum and dad really loved each other. That should make the world go round. But not for this strange and poor child whose parents could only afford the one new pair of shoes for her per year, and those at the start of the Autumn school term, resulting in the relentless teasing from the other kids. How hard it was to be on the outside of love all the time. To yearn to be in that inner circle. But it simply never happened. And while her parents carried on loving each other she carried on bouncing around the outside of their happiness, much like a minor arc on their steady circumference.

Perhaps this is why she fails at every relationship. She didn't want to be that sweet, strong, kind soul others kept describing her as, she's simply not that woman. Take the little girl away from the sarcasm, the smile, and the clever words, the everything, could we please see Holly as she really is. And that's what Susie said she did. To anyone that listened, as Susie did not know how not to share things.

Susie thought she had seen through Holly very early on. She told Holly things that were designed to either control her or to make her howl out loud. When she spoke at her wedding Holly said no matter how bad your day had been, Susie's was invariably worse, but she would tell you her tale in such a way that you would laugh out loud and go home feeling a lot better. At your expense. Obviously.

You see later on when their children had grown some more, they continued to swap many notes and didn't feel so bad when they realised they were in a similar position.

They became each other's support group. And Holly always had the upper hand. Her children were always that much less troublesome and more successful than Susie's. And better looking, said the feminist to herself. Not one to judge on appearances of course.

It was almost as though to measure herself in any way, she had to do it against the person who mattered more to her than either of them knew back then. But now she knows. It doesn't make it better.

One long summer many years ago, before they spilt up from their children's fathers Susie and Holly went away for a weekend. They went South, staying on the sea front at a lovely hotel in Dartmouth, and Susie was determined to eat a cream tea.

Holly didn't remember much more than that, other than she recalled Susie actually took a whole weekend off from man-hunting to find this cream tea. What made them so different? Susie was open about her desires; Holly was grateful for any love. Grateful even for the man who had tried to kill her. You can be the judge and jury, should you be so without sin yourself.

That night, before Holly met with Jonathan again, she tried to talk to Susie once more. She asked her if she was doing okay. And she didn't hear back. *Quid pro quo.*

THE FIRST FUMBLING

Jonathan apparently had really intended to phone me, he told me later, but a last-minute panic call from *Interpol* had him heading for Budapest instead. Individual men's size nine shoes were washing up against a particular dining experience on the Danube. Random left feet later appeared in various public bins along the many tram routes – shouting out to be paired up.

I really had intended to call Jonathan too, as even though I didn't feel I owed him anything, I was now becoming a little fascinated and possibly a little bit scared about the big 'secret'.

But I didn't make contact with him either and so even more weeks passed.

In the end neither of us called each other. I kept meaning to, but I was desperately trying to find more paid work, as the divorce lawyers weren't favouring me in this particular fiscal period, if anything their vagueness and subterfuge was clouding the actual conscious-uncoupling. And so I didn't ask Jonathan the reason why he hadn't been in touch when we eventually ran into each other at a mutual friend's charity ball. I attended on my own, which was becoming more than a habit, and he was talking to a predator from Susie's old stomping ground.

'Hey you', I said, and he looked pleased to see me. He introduced the neighbour, but I couldn't be bothered to make small talk.

I immediately took his hand and led him away from her and into the raised garden where I could have described the night-time scent from the fragrant orange blossom's and the chirruping songs from those bastard biting insects, but I'd rather tell you something else.

I kissed his cheek and then hugged him. Don't ask me why, maybe I had to make him want me and not the neighbour. He held me for a comfortable moment, more than the recommended etiquette's guide of two seconds, then he said he had to apologise.

'Oh, get lost' I said. 'Apologise for your wife, my mad best friend, leaving us alone together? She would be howling at us right now!!'

Jonathan was looking at me as though seeing me clearly for the first time.

'Fill me in then,' I carried on, annoyingly, 'is the house a tip? Got a drug den going yet? Are you being a good mum to those kids, or do you want me to kill them for you?'

And he replied by sharing things that really matter apparently. No drug den, such a relief. That Susie's kids have had to learn really quickly – he still hasn't heard back from Andrew with regards to their moving back in with him.

He's telling me about branching out on his own, and offering his services internationally, Australia initially, he loved the people and the coffee in Melbourne, and then perhaps go world-wide. He even asked my opinion.

And when I never gave it, I think that was when he understood my relationship with Susie. Susie talked and talked, and I would sometimes listen.

Maybe that's why our surface friendship seemed to work for such a long time. Susie would talk about everything and everybody and I would only give an opinion if she asked – and then only if she had given me one, to reinforce her viewpoint. She was very opinionated.

And then I see that Jonathan is also looking for some validation, does he want my advice and praise? I am so dense.

All of this time I was confused with my mixed thinking of: 'shit, how can he be so pleased to see me?'

Didn't he realise that arse of a neighbour was Susie's old arch-rival number one? God, men are so stupid at times. And yet he is sharing all of his bloody problems and dreams – get over yourself Jonathan – I gave up emotions a long time and deal only with balance sheets and business growth. And now what? Dinner? Again?

And so, even though I've told myself on more than one occasion to help convince myself that I don't like the guy, and I don't get impressed with fancy restaurants any more (he unknowingly booked the same veggie place where Iain had proposed to me all that time ago – it's changed mafia drug lords a few times since) and as I hate to drive as much as I like to drink (the original reason for Dr Harry's haphazard coping therapy requirements as dictated by Iain, apparently I got narky and aggressive when drunk), here I am squeezing in to my only decent little black dress and calling Daniella to see if she would like to drop me into town.

I like to think power, but I certainly don't like to think sex.

I could see through the huge window that Jonathan is waiting for me in the pre-Baroque anti-room of this famously expensive restaurant as Daniella kicks me out of the passenger door. After three hefty gin and tonics I could heal the whole world mama.

Fortunately, he's waiting in the wings, so as long as I smile and aim straight at him…

(Jonathan: If I say she looked stunning then I'd be lying. She turns heads and she has no clue. She smiles that always hovering pink-gummy smile, directed at me, and I can see the hopes of all of the men in my peripheral vision fade away. She walks straight up to me, side-lined only for a moment by someone who thinks he knows her, and gives me the biggest hug.)

The evening went so well. I am an expert at doing this. I made him laugh often, made him feel important by listening to his every word, injecting some of my own recently researched objective opinions on his work. I introduced some current affairs stuff to assert my intellect and then I gin-morphed into his dead wife. And of course, I went home with him, it was always going to happen.

The sex was predictably awful, but then that's never been my strong point. And I take some comfort about that because I think he is now in love with me, or at least knows another side of me. Bloody stupid man. Bloody stupider me.

The following morning my gin depression reminded me that I'd slept with him.

Shit. I slept with my best friend's husband. And it was gross. And now he loves me. Great. Who was it that said: 'I am very conscious that I am not very wise at all'? Me, I think.

THE SEX THERAPIST AND HOLLY

Dr Palmer was well aware that Mrs H wasn't keen on sex at all. Early on in Harriet's attempts at structured sessions, with sex being such a pivotal part in every person's lives, whether married, in a long-term relationship or just a grab-and-go, thank you ma'am, she 'discovered' this reticence. And as there are more reasons and explanations than a one-stop-shop methodology to 'fix' any problem, Harriet had wanted to get to the sacral root of Holly's fear of intimacy. Intimacy avoidance, she had read recently, and therefore she typically wanted to test-run this idea out on who she wrongly-thought was her most vulnerable client.

'I'm not scared of intimacy for God's sake; I just don't like sex.' Holly had said.

'And I don't need to do any of those bloody psycho tests either' she shouted to her therapist as Harriet bounded out of the room to race to her printer.

'I can't be bothered.' But Dr Harry didn't believe this. She told her client that it was because she was insecure about her body. 'I'm not' defended the poor woman who had always known that her therapist mostly practised on her.

Harriet was in full flow now. 'One reason is that we women have been conditioned through the ages to not like our bodies. Forget the minds and how smart we are – it's all about the body.

'We compare ourselves to the actresses and models, and we're bombarded by the messages from the hoardings everywhere telling us we are not good enough – look at those rough armpits Holly!

127

'Look at your hair! Your boobs aren't big enough! Your bum isn't pert enough! Your moustache needs threading, that cellulite will turn stomachs.' She could have been describing herself.

Men, on the other hand, thought Holly, had so far avoided the relentless barrage of the not-quite-good-enough propaganda machine dressed as PR, but their lack of self-worth is catching up faster than they realise.

Holly didn't have a moustache; she had a lovely Iranian girl who worked in the Turkish barbers in the Chinese quarter to sort that out. And whilst her boobs and hips showed she had borne children, they were okay. Her figure may yet still turn a few heads, if that was what she wanted. As for her armpits, well, more often than not Holly's cardigan covered her arms so Dr Harry really couldn't voice an opinion on those. Not that it stopped her.

The sex conversation was attempted more than once. Aural sex Holly said, as she didn't want to listen anymore, and tried to deflect away from the subject, after all, this made her feel very uncomfortable. A good therapist would ask Holly to keep revisiting the physical response to this avoidance, usually centred in the stomach, second brain, gut instinct and all that, to put the emotion into perspective. But as we already know, Harriet didn't fit that description, and we understood that her own limited sexual experiences were mortifying, so she used these sessions for her own self-gratification. Harriet's quick fix for feeling better about her own failures with sex.

Some deep-rooted repulsion may be the answer for Holly's dread, she insisted, and fear it most certainly is of intimacy, attempting to misplace more false memories. Maybe a disgusting old uncle patting her bottom inappropriately, possibly the top-shelf non- glamour magazines pushing an acceptable glimpse of female abuse, seen when she was so vulnerable and before the publishers were ordered to blacken the covers.

It may have been the exclusion from her parents' happiness. Harriet had persisted with that idea, perhaps to protect her from her own pain, or maybe Holly would not be defined by using sex as a weapon. Possibly it was as the result of childbirth. Two children after all. Or maybe, just maybe, and while Dr Harry didn't like this one, and Susie argued against it more than once, Holly simply couldn't be bothered to draw attention to herself.

This resulted in Harriet's bastardisation of *Banksy's* fine words, something along the lines of:

'The Advertisers. Leering at you from tall buildings to make you feel so small, without asking your opinion to push home your inadequacies. Making flippant comments from bus graphics implying you're not sexy enough, and that all the fun is happening somewhere else. You owe nothing. Less than nothing. They owe you everything for making you feel like this'.

She finally shut up to take a much-needed deep breath and looked at Holly. Bill Haley had crept back onto her lap and took advantage of Holly's automatic stroking to defuse the tension.

She looked directly back at her would-be brainwasher.

'Honestly doc, I seriously am more than happy with myself. I am just not that keen on sex. I don't need fixing. But thank you for trying,' she said, in that lovely insecure way she gave out.

*

On her way home she thought she heard her lovely departed dad whisper: Stop listening to all that rubbish Holly. Fall in love first.

SHOW HIM THE MONEY TRAIL

Iain Hastings knew the simple rules of divorce for a man. You hand over your money and you don't get access to your children. But this one was going to be very hard to sweep under the stickiest of the 1960s cream shag-pile carpet in the office of the house-master at the borstal where he'd spent his formative years. Not least as there definitely were legitimate children involved this time, but also as his latest, and soon to be ex-wife for good, had a rather faithful ally who had fought most of his or her cartoon life on a range of subjects and with a range of enemies.
And this cross-dressing confidant wasn't about to let Holly give up on a well-deserved pay-out, and a roof over her head. If not the one she lived in now, then an even bigger one.
He knew the rules of divorce inside out, and he really did not want this one. If asked, he would have said he had loved her. Even admired her. And really didn't want to let her go.
Hastings normally gave a good brief and a hefty retainer to his regular multi-tasking lawyer, who by now totally understood that his client did not lose in any deal or with any woman.
But Hastings hadn't told that particular agent about the underlying caveat in this specific battle, so he decided to use his other go-to firm, one that he had trusted a long time ago for a one-off situation, a confidentiality issue, a family problem, if you like.
This professional outfit was based in the city centre and Iain Hastings could have the face-to-face conversations that were needed.

He really hoped he may be able to manipulate his way out of something that he had justified in his own mind as an error of judgement, well, two errors, maybe three, but this was something that had the potential to bite him very hard. After all, the regular outgoings could be seen as blackmail and be used against him further in his financial fight with Holly and, please, everyone remember, no-one ever beats Iain Hastings in the money game.

Added to all of the recent setbacks, his importing of hollowed out coffee beans refilled with heroin being shipped via Italy (he'd imported this particular bean for a long time and Lloyds continued to be happy to facilitate this type of bill of lading, it made them a lot of money after all, and so he was always above suspicion), his foray into county lines management, viciously cutting out the next line of foot soldiers, had now attracted some local law enforcement interest. This drug import business was hugely profitable and added to his already inflated income. He knew how to hide the money too (lots of borders in the UK, his wife's many bank accounts, plenty of students happy to supplement their educational costs by allowing the use of their bank accounts too, and with the help of some insider bank staff, the students didn't always need to know their accounts were being used).

Itch was simply just too arrogant to realise the real risk, systemic or otherwise, of drug running.

He had also made the rookie mistake of sampling the goods, to keep him top dog in his bona fide day job.

Every other Cartel chief would have said this was definitely a no-no. A guaranteed slippery slope. Hasting's days in Colombia as the leading Trust-fund investor had greatly paved the way for garnering the knowledge, and how to disguise the goods and to transport these via Europe, as they appreciate their coffee. An added benefit of hiding the trail. Iain was a sad, going-to-seed and rich old banker. Not some glamorous drug lord. This 'patch' although still profitable, was shrinking. Due in part to the coveting by much smarter and violent street kids; including his own off-spring it would later appear.

However, in the beginning he had been excited about this way of making extra cash. And he was smart enough to know how to place and layer the funds in the banking world if he needed to, with some legitimate money-laundering into the trust accounts of his many children, to be held there until they were of legal age. And many more non-legitimate ways of getting the dirty money back into its laundered state, at any cost. Without any trace back to himself. Not always a smart move if you think you are going to get into a money fight with your even smarter wife.

Hastings had kept a gun, legally, and the license supported his pigeon problem, and the occasional domestic pet, he liked neither cats nor dogs, but he had never once fired it at a person.

He had a large warehouse where the stolen vehicles could be spray painted (usually dove-grey, nicely anonymous) and 'borrowed' number plates exchanged with a smooth regularity.

And he had a team of lieutenants who didn't need to know his name. These boys ran their own gangs of wannabes who recruited users and stole on demand from old people, their own parent's houses, out of cars, school children, he genuinely didn't care. Although he kept an eye out on one of the runners, as they were loosely related and he could see the boy was using the goods and losing the plot. Hastings had just the one friend who he trusted implicitly, mostly because he had dirt on him which would have ruined his career should the photographs and videos and other supporting documents ever fall into the wrong hands. Especially his wife's. Iain Hastings made an appointment with this friend, Manny Sarr, a struck-off solicitor, at the offices of the Law Society central Birmingham, for the week following Susie's death.

DAN-GEROUS LIAISONS

Daniella Ingle loved to listen and she loved to talk, to all and sundry. She listened carefully to the elderly people who came to her gym and coffee shop. She chatted to the sweet and much under-valued and under-paid carers. She talked to the pastry delivery-man who admittedly was a little bit terrified of her at the same time as being a little bit in love with her, which confused him greatly. She talked to the daughters of those elderly, and their grand-daughters too, and they all loved that she really did listen. That, without a doubt, was one of her best skills.

She would hear many stories of when her clients were younger. Their dreams and unfulfilled ambitions; their confidences, who would have guessed the elderly knew and had enjoyed so many Karma Sutras' positions! These ladies loved to share their memories, and their rather disturbing sex lives, with this weirdly fascinating and beautiful woman.

One particular confidant, Kaddy Sarr, garrulous as her native country-folk are, once she got over the shock of realising Daniella was as weird as her son, had started to confide in her a lot, after discovering that they had a mutual friend. Mister *Itchy* Hastings. More than a general acquaintance to Kaddy, she knew him from her London days, all of those years ago, she said.

Initially, Daniella had tried to distance herself from this association, as Kaddy could take up an awful lot of her time, and she generally spoke in riddles.

But with Holly wanting her to find anything, (anything at all please Daniella) to pre-empt Susie's Will fiasco, she had it confirmed that Hastings really couldn't keep it in his trousers for anything and anyone throughout all of his many liaisons, from London around the whole world, Kaddy said.

He'd had at least four marriages to her knowledge. She knew so much about Hastings that Daniella had told her if she was anyone else she would have been locked away for stalking the poor chap.

When this lady's bubbly and completely exhausted carer came over, that very last time, Daniella realised a huge chunk of Kaddy's recollection was missing and now she knew she needed to hear more.

The conversation had run in the usual old-lady ways. In and out of her subject matter, and what a nice cat she once had, then about her keepsakes from her days working in London, back to Hastings and his philandering charms, a hard desk and some videos in her loft, Daniella thought she said, and Hasting's blackmailing ways. Back to the cat.

Daniella would have liked to have carried on with that tittle-tattle, maybe a one-to-one without her other duties, but the carer's agency charged strictly by the hour (and that included travelling time) and being on minimum wage even if she had wanted to stay and chat, she couldn't. Or wouldn't, as there's only so much old-people-listening you can pretend to engage in.

The following week when the old lady didn't turn up for the fitness sessions, or the free coffee and gossip, Daniella was informed by the carer (who admirably had more than one bitter and twisted old soul to look after and was already introducing another lonely senior citizen to a new way of exercise, as recommended by his GP) that the old Gambian bully had died.

As with any of her deceased clients and subject to getting an invitation, Daniella would always attend the funerals. She had five outfits that she successfully rotated. And so, on that particular day she was wearing a bolero dress, complete with black sequins, hand sown, with the sexiest pink net petticoat peeking from below the skirt. Her polished plain black Cowboy boots she wore to every memorial service. Daniella threw a pink wrap over her shoulders as an homage to Kaddy, as she knew this old lady had loved her bright touches, and matched her lipstick accordingly.

It was always the subtle things that she remembered about others that made people gravitate to her.

And gravitate they did. Firstly, the old lady's very tall, fairly dark, very handsome, and obviously very fascinated son, who she had caught sight of on the rare occasions he dropped his mother at the gym. He held her hand for a long time as he thanked her for coming and complimented her on her stunning outfit and suggested dinner or coffee. Perhaps a weekend away?

Then the carer, Becky, who may still have been on the clock, and possibly had to short-change another client, or have her money docked by the local authorities, had nonetheless made the effort to attend, and the time to root out Daniella.

'She was very excited about being able to talk to you' said the lovely Becky, about the jolly old dead lady.

'She was going to find all the bits and bobs about him, he had so many skeletons she used to tell me, her son had told her he stored extra stuff at the house when he still lived there. But then she fell over the stupid deaf cat on the stairs coming down from the loft.'

Having never met this evil feline, though she had heard many of his stories from both Susie and Holly, Daniella solemnly asked after the wellbeing of the expert therapist, Bill Haley.

'Oh, she squashed him', Becky said. 'It was while she was digging his grave that her heart went out.'

Daniella called Holly shortly after the funeral party had finally exited to the pub. She just had to share the cat story and that of the new man, Manny, with whom she had arranged to meet the next day, just for coffee but not at her place.

She didn't want to demasculate him just yet. And he reminded her of someone, she just couldn't quite put her finger on it.

But, typically, as per the nine-times-out-of-ten rule that Susie and Daniella put in place, Holly's phone went unanswered.

NOT ON THE LIST, YOU CAN'T COME IN

Not many people are aware, if they cared at all,
about the amount of data that is kept on every single
one of us. Whether we've ever been in trouble or
not, went over the speed limit, stole a sweet from
those on display at Woolworths, or having dipped,
unintentionally, into our overdrafts. Which would beg
a bigger question: who polices the police?
The constant surveillance recording in real-time on
the streets, listening in on the time-saving devices
we happily pay over the odds for, and install in the
most private of rooms, the baby's nursery, the
bedroom. The bathrooms. Paying to be spied on.
'*Alexa*, where the fuck are the wipes?'
Never mind the Big Brothers watching our spending
habits under the cover of loyalty cards. Oh, you have
liver cancer do you? Your spending habits showed
you bought far too much wine. Sorry, the NHS won't
help you, but now we've got your DNA. Result.
Little Holly Hastings was on the domestic-abuse-
victims list. Her doctor had been obligated to share
this knowledge after finally acknowledging the
Practice Nurse's concerns that no-one could fall that
many times without something being medically
wrong. However, the GP wasn't obligated to report
the name of the suspected abuser. More's the pity.
Susie was on the sexually transmitted disease list
more than once. The confidential service has a
responsibility to monitor the spread of STI's and her
name wasn't redacted.
She was also on the domestic-abuse-abusers list.

The Social Workers may have been over-stretched, but they knew when they needed to protect their jobs too. Susie might have been listed only the once by them (following their box-ticking visit) but this was added to later, by the doctor treating the second-degree burns on Tommy's hand.

And still her name would remain on this register long after her death. If any of her children went off the rails then this would be a good, solid and supportive reason to show why they did.

From her days in *Her Majesty's Service* and through-out her transition, whenever Daniella travelled, she was on some country or other's radar.

Daniella was on the majority of military watch lists. International. Her skills with ISIL had marked her out as someone to be developed and thrown into even more dangerous situations, she was a natural born killer, honed by hatred of herself back then, and the unkindness she was nurtured with. Except she developed into this wonderful woman instead, therefore rendering her useless in general.

We can't win the equal rights issues over here, she had said to Holly, so no chance of an intersex person being taken seriously in any war zone.

Her early trips to Thailand were duly registered, whilst in themselves not against any Queens or Country, and in her case always to support and validate herself and were certainly not for her to join in any political protests.

She valued her freedom after all, and those Bangkok jails were not the typical Koh Samui hotel standards.

And so, on every passport scan out of the UK there would be another addition into the do-not-reply email account monitored by persons stationed in a deep underground bunker, not far from the official listening doughnut headquarters in Cheltenham. These would eventually be manually added to a database about her specific junkets, but usually only as and when they needed to clear the inbox out. Government cuts did not allow for unnecessary expenditure such as email vault space.

Sometimes these emails went into the nonsecure backup *Cloud* without having been read or reviewed. This is pretty standard procedure for most bureaucracies.

The trip to the USA was one that wasn't missed. This had been rapidly shared with the relevant and interested, though not joined-up, Central Intelligence agencies, just in case she was going to out-trump Trump (whom she was actually very fond of, having once been touched up by him when she was accidentally not vetted and labelled correctly. He had the biggest shock).

And as a result of this email ping, throughout all of her time there and strangely unnoticed by Daniella and her ex-FBI colleague, they were followed by one of those agencies.

From the airport, to the old crime scene and back to the ranch – picking up some excited chatter along the way, as the listening devices used by the Intelligence services nowadays don't need to be placed anywhere near the subject.

All of their actions were documented and filed away in yet another deep underground bunker in Nevada, under a desert better known for space invaders. Exact location unknown, but the coffee was reputed to be excellent. A particularly fine double-roasted coffee bean, *Sidamo*. With a smattering of heroin dust.

Kaddy Sarr was also on a register. As a shining example of an illegal immigrant, she had worked hard, paid some taxes (that was on another list where she had made top ranking) one would wonder why something hadn't been done about her. It may be possible that those doing the watching were after bigger fry.

Whilst Kaddy was still cleaning in London, she could have had access to confidential files from the Stock Brokers' offices that ought to have been shredded but instead these may have been kept for herself in case she needed any leverage. She'd shagged one of theirs after all, caught many times on the in-house security cameras.

This is all supposition, of course. We never know why we have a file, or what is in it, but it is always useful to keep some dirt on others. We all know about the favour bank; this was Kaddy's reverse of that. For reasons unclear, she found out that resisting arrest is a crime. Even if you are not told why you are being arrested. Kaddy understood this on too many occasions, being black.

Her son however, ought to have been arrested many times and for the right reasons, and locked away forever.

He was on multiple international registers.

Not only for his sexual perversions, his public order offences, and the suspicion of him being on the edge of a drug cartel. Although that one was yet to be proven. The list was huge. His removal from his legal standing, after his employer came under pressure to disbar him, was not public knowledge unless someone knew how to do a very deep search, but it was on a government register. Along with all of the other sex offenders they had in their own cross-party ranks, those that had kept their jobs.

The senior partner at his old company had allowed Manlafi Sarr to stay in an administration role of an autonomous division, he wasn't to be associated with the main partnership, as this ownership was confused with many layers and significant controllers and anonymous Trusts and it would stay that way. No dirt needed to draw attention to such. He had kept Manny close, mainly because he was a font of legal knowledge and, more importantly perhaps, fabulous in the sack, if you knew which way to turn. Manlafi Sarr was watched more closely that his mother. *Bigger Fish to Catch* was the rubbed-out pencil note on his file.

Jonathan, the famous but steady forensic podiatrist was also on a register, and this was one where all of the Global agencies happily pulled together. As they all might need his particular expertise at some stage. And while there may have been a notation on his file after one investigation in the USA, some evidence having been misplaced or something, by all means they got the right result and as that was such a minor thing, they edited this notation out in a future version.

The original account stayed as it was, now filed
under sand dust at yet another undisclosed, and not
airtight, storage facility.
Dr Harry had also come to the attention of other
interested agencies. Probably more to do with her
marriage to Manlafi Sarr, a known sex offender, as
they just couldn't catch him 'in the act'. Or possibly
her alcohol consumption (she had noticed her recycling box had been moved on more than one
occasion, but had put it down to the many city foxes,
as they are known to have a fondness for chasing
down the urban, wild, wheelie bins, who loved a drop
of rancid dustbin dregs). This could also have been
as a result of the General Medical Council who,
whilst constantly working against a backlog of more
than twelve months, really did not like their ex-GPs
to still be inappropriately using their qualifications in
non-pre-approved career moves. Hence why the
GMC always have a mountain of paperwork,
continually searching the minutia for something to
hang themselves with.
It was more than likely that the reason the failed,
flabby old frump, Dr Palmer that is, came up so
often, was because she was on these lists solely
because she was a common denominator for others
on other agencies lists.
And some poor misguided fool is employed to find
patterns, mostly where they just do not exist.
Government job creation; for their own little families.
Iain Hastings had been recorded on the radar since
it was still a paper list, long before the migration to
last century's spreadsheets.

144

A ledger normally associated with sales and purchases, accounts and receivables, cross-referenced with dates and contacts.

Some of this information was inevitably lost when the entries had been manually copied over to the new databases, as in true corporate fashion the 'best fit to purpose' software being already out of date, and the temp who was doing the transcribing hadn't been shown the importance of the many code words and abbreviations.

The original documents would have been stored, somewhere, but not shredded. Iain Hastings was a lucky so-and-so.

WHEN DANIELLA MET SUSIE

Susie had clearly sharpened her innate understanding of the importance of divide and conquer from the many abuses in her early life, and for the necessary protection of her many adult versions. She had multiple personas. Holly Hastings was her longest-running friend, one that she had nurtured easily from early on outside the gates at nursery school collection times. They would snuggle close together discussing the other mothers and the apparent failings of the other children. To be fair, Susie would be the one criticising and Holly would shame her, as all women have got to stop being so harsh on their own gender.

One person who neither of them could either offend or need to defend was Holly's newest client, Daniella. And Susie knew she needed to divide and conquer this one, to keep Holly as her own best friend. No sharing here.

In the spirit of every surviving Mafia Godfather, with enemies closer and all that, Susie called Daniella and suggested they may need to plan an attack for rescuing their joint friend, Holly. Regardless of what they thought they were rescuing her from, and without either of them questioning if she really did need to be rescued, there had to be an opening gambit. And they both accepted this without further ado.

Now, we know Daniella wasn't anyone's fool, except for bad taste in lovers and maybe some off-the-wall Cowboy boots, but she may have been equally as fascinated by Holly's tales about Susie as Susie had been about Daniella's.

Nothing cruel, but some laugh out loud tales that most probably were not true.

Both thought a good joint bitching session as an interrogation may just work. Daniella accepted the invitation with good grace and agreed to host Susie at her new Boho coffee shop within *CP Fitness.* Which was exactly what Susie had intended.

Evidently neither had thought to mention this to Holly. For her own good, perhaps, or it may have been an unconscious act on both of their parts. Coincidence.

But still, Holly was a good excuse for them to meet their adversaries. The passive, but not common, denominator.

Daniella, hair freshly trimmed and tinted on that same morning, wearing her glorious statement outfit of swirls and primary colours, met Susie in her everyday absolute gorgeous gloriousness, single non-primary colour, one size too small, green costume with matching fake handbag and white wedges, on that perfect Wednesday morning.

'Hump-day,' said Susie, as openers.

Daniella made sure she was the hostess sublime. She had pre-ordered the full-fat pastries from her confused pastry deliveryman, who was still a little bit in love with her, as she had already determined that Susie would not want anything slightly vegan.

These were presented, as though freshly baked in the kitchens, onto the exclusive hand-sanded and second-hand wooden table (Eco and up-cycled. Holly would love this, said Susie).

The croissants nicely warm and oozing with butter-crumbling deliciousness, the choc au pain melting in front of your eyes.

Piping hot coffee and steamed raw milk for Susie.
Daniella knew the importance of hospitality.
When she spoke with the *Elders* back in The Levant,
she (then he) knew how to honour and support their
obvious superiority. She would hold the nod down as
she served the well-mashed foul black tea. She had
broken the foot-bread with humility, closing her eyes
during the prayers to whichever loving and all-seeing
God accounted for the infidel's man-made sins (war
not included). She would back away with eyes still
lowered, not threatening, whilst subtly trying to
dodge the constant spittle of Afghani-black nicotine
and tea.
She learned a lot from her time fighting the invisible
enemy. The henchmen and thy spit.
Susie, fortunately, didn't spit too much and wasn't in
need of humility. She was loud, she was diverting,
she was fun and she hid behind many acts,
developed over many years. Her fresh new one had
become her latest appropriated performance
(essence of Kaddy, of all people), and with it, her
host could glimpse the see-through persona.
On the surface she did not appear easily led,
although she could give the effect if it suited the
occasion, much like she could borrow any
personality to make fun of a situation.
It may be prudent to note at this juncture that Susie
also had a cunning brain and therefore should not
have been underestimated.

And whilst the initial excuse to meet up was to discuss how best to look after little Holly, after all, it had been a few years since Iain tried to throttle her and still, she had not received any hint of the settlement she deserved; they instead veered from people in common to children, moving from lovers (none shared) and lots of gossip, picking over each other's perceptions and flaws to store away for any further manipulation.

Daniella warmed to the idea of a lovely new friendship, one so totally different from her confidante, Holly.

She noted Susie's speech patterns, and mimicked these accordingly to get Susie to trust in her.

Daniella saw Susie reflecting her own mannerisms, and recognised how they mirrored each other in other ways not intended.

Susie would later borrow Daniella's fashion sense and idiosyncrasies, which would confuse the life out of Holly and Jonathan. And then Daniella would kindly create some more.

Daniella, after all, was the coach.

TOMMY IS LOST

Tommy really missed his mum. He had all the usual raging torments of being a teenager way before she had gone to answer her last phone call. Long since he was an acne-ridden thirteen-year-old, but add this emptiness on top of everything and he was a ticking time-bomb. Mind you, his skin was so much better since she had died and Holly had stopped the dairy products. Maybe it had cleared up due to a little gentleness. There wasn't much kindness in his younger days.

Tommy had never wanted to move into the remote and knackered old wreck of a cottage, even after his mum had spent a fortune making it all show-room fine and fancy. She even changed the thatch on the roof to clay tiles to stop the 'cats and dogs raining down' that she constantly teased Holly's dog with. The dog paid little regard to this. Tommy resented that soft dog too, and the attention his mother gave to her, regularly kicking her when no-one was watching, one time breaking her jaw. Holly didn't let the broken Cocker Spaniel stay there again after that.

Tommy didn't particularly like Jonathan, but didn't try to kick him. Tommy had never liked his own dad all that much either, to be honest. Why hadn't he come for him and his sister?

Mind you, Abby didn't want to move in with their dad. Abby was more settled at their latest home, she even did the cooking and washing now, for all of them, with some disasters.

Their dad's new and much younger wife was not like his fun mum at all. She was smart and a bit dumpy. A plain and frumpy obstetrician-gynaecologist at a specialist hospital many miles away from them.

Mum used to rip it out of their dad at every given opportunity, about how his standards had dropped. The OBGYN would talk about adding to their little family unit whenever Tommy and Abby had gone to visit, and she had made them proper dinners too, lots of nutrition, but no meat though as she was 'against all cruelty'. Not like his mum. She loved the cruelty. Dinner was always by invitation only though, as their potential step-mum also filled in at the Central Hospital for Ladies in London, and cancellations were to be avoided at all costs. It just wasn't the 'done' thing, she said. Neither child questioned why they couldn't see their dad outside of this arrangement.

Tommy always made sure that he'd drank some vodka from Jonathan's cellar before the formal visits. Although he wasn't too sure the wine cellar should be called that as it was just two steps down from the freezing pantry.

Grey Goose and whacky baccy were already a daily habit and just wouldn't cut it today.

He'd had to report to his new boss (in the year below him at his old school, to add to the insult) about his failing targets, and he really couldn't be bothered to stand outside yet another school trying to give the appearance of waiting for yet another younger brother who 'must have scarpered earlier, he does this all of the time'.

Sometimes the mothers would look at Tommy's broken veins in his once white eyes and note the scabbed and painful red sores around his nose, and occasionally feel sorry for him.

But mostly they ignored him, pulling their own children closer to them while turning their backs to him, giving him dirty looks over their shoulders.

With every right too; he didn't even notice them.

And so here was Tommy the innocent trying to hook even more children in with his smiles and the sweets and the sugar-coated pills. A man's got to earn a living.

Tommy the innocent, as his mum had once called him after finding him with the keys to her car in his trouser pocket, denying he'd driven it even when she had made him touch the engine, keeping his hand there until it burnt quite badly. This boy just wants to try and forget.

Only yesterday he had asked to borrow one of the 'company cars' so he could go and experiment a little farther out of town.

He even attempted to meet the big boss at the warehouse on the run-down industrial estate, but had only got far enough in to see one of his old vehicles being given a new lease of life before being sold back into the legitimate motor trade to an unsuspecting buyer.

He hadn't been allowed further in, nor indeed was he allowed to use that particular van again, not since the last run into Birmingham where he'd got a right old ding in the front, the red flakes of paint were in the process of being bashed out yet.

That Transit had been put away in storage for a while, too old and expensive to bother to repair and too hot to handle, even with the newest fake plates. He couldn't recall too much about that day, more of a horrible dream. He only found out when some police officers came round to Jonathan's house, later that same night, that his mum had died on the *Aston Expressway* that morning.

Tommy had to become a recruiter and rise up the ranks. He needed to make more money, to run a team, to manage his staff with pills and beatings and bribes.

He knew where the bodies were buried, he used to brag to his old school mates, the former *First Fluffy Feathers* gang, most of them having given up on him by now, but the few left were still impressed with the designer belts and the gaudy wheel trims on his latest pimped and uninsured car. His mum had dealt with all of that paperwork stuff for him.

Tommy genuinely missed the familiarity of the misplaced love, and the torment of the pain dished out by his mum.

THE EMOTIONAL THERAPIST AND SUSIE

Dr Harriet Palmer, after yet another long night of hot
flushes, flashbacks and too much warm, white, but
no longer bargain-basement New World wine (when
will she learn to get up and put the bottle back in her
fridge?), covered up her ever-increasing bulk with
the sadness deep-rooted within that old shabby
dressing gown, and performed her usual morning
rituals. Slamming the lavatory door loudly enough to
wake the dead, before the grief of realisation hit her
that both of the pains in her life, well, two out of
three, were no longer available to trigger her excuse
for drinking.
No glistening or stinking black shit in the litter tray,
just maybe a vague wee-whiff from times gone,
human or cat, who would know. No reason now to
try and keep Bill Haley and his psychic skills away
from Susie, who would doubtless be late.
She had watched her wedding video again on that
morning and decided that a big enough hint had
been planted and she would destroy this today.
After showing it to Susie, maybe.
Picking up the post from the day before yesterday's
delivery, noting the return addresses of the General
Medical Council on each envelope had stayed the
same.
She'd had many 'invitations' to talk about her false
practise. These most recent summons she now put
back down again on the stained kitchen table-cloth,
as she reached across some dead Cyclamen plant
to open the sash window, knocking the painted pot
onto the floor and briefly thinking about having to sell
the family home.

She thought about where she would have liked to relocate, and if she wanted to carry on practicing with a smaller client base.

She may have pondered a move out of her safe and familiar area, and thought maybe she ought to retire now, before she opened the post and faced those consequences. Perhaps she could buy herself a small-holding in a remote part of Wales, possibly around the Herefordshire border (at that time it was still relatively affordable if you kept far south of Shropshire) and keep free-to-range chickens, for their eggs only. Well, maybe enough for herself and if there were any surplus she could always sell them to cover their food costs. Get herself an honesty box. And set up a recording camera to watch the thieves. She could even start to make organic jam from the fruit shrubs in the newly visualised perfect garden, where nothing ever dies. She would call the jam artisan, as people buy into that. But we won't know which direction her thoughts would take, as Susie, for once, was very early, and clearly in need of more attention than usual.

'I've told him I'm going to tell her' she announced loudly, as soon as she flung the kitchen door wide open, without knocking first, and before the much-needed beans were added to her newly purchased coffee machine.

The weakness from so many years of self-loathing, her marriage and career failings, along with the resentment of the Sarr's and hatred of herself in general, had finally taken a huge emotional toll on Harriet Palmer.

Without any time for her versions of preparing for her clients, no loud music, nor a silent nod or waiting for permission to speak, just a straightforward invasion of this woman's privacy, was it really any surprise that Dr Harry turned right back at Susie virtually shouting: 'And what exactly do you think that will achieve?'

The burden of her own shortcomings and the dark energies of others, along with not being able to put herself into the toughened protection that was her usual routine before seeing clients, brought the real and defensive Harriet to the surface. Perhaps we ought to realise that even therapists lose their heads too.

Dr Harry had just buried her mother-in-law and whilst that may not, in itself, have caused this unusual retort, it made her understand the grief process so much more clearly. She felt actual pain, for once.

The woman had so obviously hated her. She had blamed her for Manlafi preferring lady-boys, well, anyone other than her really, but she stayed in Harriet's home as though she had every right, taunting her on many occasions, and on the others, entertaining her daughter-in-law greatly.

Kaddy would share her life stories and some of the histories of the characters she had met along the way. The jolly black girl used to be such fun.

And Harriet Palmer, stupid, fat, worn-out Harriet Palmer, missed her companion.

Susie, of course, didn't notice this reaction from Harry, as Susie's focus was only ever about Susie and who was giving her the most attention.

In her own defence, she would have said, she only spoke the words out loud just to test them, and anyway, what harm would it really do?

Big, brash, spoilt Susie, who thought about no-one but herself and her desires, appeared to be perfectly prepared and happy to ruin her best friend's life. And maybe she genuinely would have done, then.

Without apology, Dr Palmer pushed Mrs B into the sad, cold and unloved living room where an ancient printer sat next to a computer with its USB cable attached, and an old video player was hooked to the TV.

The older woman told her client to sit there while she went to grab some cheap, instant coffee. And Susie, for once, did as she was told.

WHOOPS, HOLLY DOES IT AGAIN

Some more days merged into weeks and I get another call from Jonathan. We agree to meet up for a drink after (his) work – I feel the call of the Alpha controlling male kick in, but for reasons totally unclear to me I managed to make sure I could be there.

We met up in a tiny little establishment where I ended up ordering something with garlic, just in case, and a huge glass of New Zealand Chardonnay, now that this wine wasn't made fun of anymore. Jonathan was still carefully reviewing the menu that he'd been studying when I had arrived, and upon my wine being brought to the table, he finally ordered the same dish as me.

He asked me how my life has been. I didn't bother asking how far back I should go but I made sure I had something other than the failed fumblings to talk about.

I said I had been doing a lot of thinking and had an epiphany about how women and men interact, and that this has proved so useful with one of my clients, (the female owner of *Mop, Shop and Crop*, who had just met a man who really wanted to look after her, materially, but this meant having to give up the successful housekeeping agency that had taken her years to build up, as he worked abroad a lot and wanted her to travel with him).

I questioned was it all really simply just about women needing men because they've been conditioned to?

Jonathan asked in what respect and I turned on him as I knew he hadn't been listening and said, 'exactly which part are you having trouble with?' As I too had learned how to be derisive, without sounding it. Hey Dad, you would have been so proud of me. 'I'm saying do women simply need to be looked after, and whether this is on a financial level, most commonly, or a physical level, though not how a man would think, why is it so wrong? Why shouldn't the sexes have individual strengths and why does it matter if a woman can state out loud that she just needs to be supported on a material level?' Jonathan looked as though he was not sure if he needed to answer this, and he didn't really attempt to, even if he had the slightest idea of what I was going on about, so instead he endeavoured to change the subject to the last time we met; subtlety, actually, was not his strength.

'Holly, can we talk about what is happening between us please, I need to get my emotions in order.'

God he's just like all the rest. I'm going all round the houses to avoid the subject of the last time we met, and he goes straight for the man question.

If I were the *Supreme Being*, I'd have refined the male of the species a few times before letting him loose on the opposite sex.

Although I must admit, I would love to be able to be more direct without constantly sounding so weakly passive. The only thing I'd inherited from my lovely soft dad.

'Jonathan' I said. 'We have to separate our feelings from Susie's wishes – what happened last weekend was, well, awkward but expected. Two people thrown together what did we think was going to happen?'
I'm certainly not going to tell him it was a bit like sleeping with my lovely soft dad (which incidentally I hadn't – but the familiarity of a friend's husband wasn't something I wanted to relive, how on earth had Susie managed to sleep with BB Brad all of that time?).
The actual physical thing wasn't any worse than I had experienced before, I was completely pissed after all, but I think I had really wanted to fall for him as Susie had pretended she had.
The emptiness left following the encounter (not perfect, been on a one-night stand more than once before I married Iain) made me dislike me even more, if that was possible.
So, in order to change the subject, as I really didn't feel comfortable getting into discussing the absolute disaster of when Holly shagged Jonathan, I asked him for some advice about my mad, migratory and inconsistent foot pain. I'd fallen into the trap of cheap and easy shoes a long time ago, following my annual new school shoe rituals, and even when I had enough money, I always thought my feet would outlive me.
He took this change of subject really well and in the relative darkness of the empty bistro, thankfully we were in a corner, he made me remove my old low-cost boots, although my mis-matched trainer socks remained firmly on, and he cradled the heel of my foot with one hand, rocking the ankle side-to-side

and rotating the whole foot, whilst pushing his fingers from the other hand into the muscles.

Much like a decent *Shiatsu* master would, testing how these movements worked with the bones and nerves.

Now, I do know a little bit about the connection with pressure points and organs, I'd read it somewhere, maybe in one of Harry's self-help magazines on the many occasions when she had kept me waiting whilst she sobered up yet again.

And I also thought I knew that this foot stuff wouldn't be some sort of trickery that Jonathan would engage in, but all the same, things that had never seen the light of day suddenly needed titanium-plated sunglasses.

At one point when he caught me looking down at his perfect hands, at his perfect face, he cleared his perfect throat and asked if I would be able to sort *Susie's* accounts out, soon, maybe this afternoon, perhaps now, if that suited me.

It really suited me.

In truth I don't recall anything much about whether the bill was paid, or the journey back to his car, back to his place.

He drove round the country lanes very quickly. I do half-recall the reusable (for once not discarded) bright orange supermarket's plastic carrier bag full of receipts, abandoned in Susie's legacy haphazard manner on her big statement and hideous work-desk, scattered onto the hastily filed bank accounts and other documentation which had been thrown in yet another bag on the floor.

And yet what I really remember is the warmth of his left hand gently at the small of my back as he guided me away from her den and shut the door to his bedroom.

I have also committed to memory the feeling of his body so close to me and I want to relive his mouth on my neck as he helped me take off my coat, my scarf, my protective armour. Removing my years of feeling-less.

I yearn still to hear his intake of breath again as he pulled my jumper over my head and pressed his face to the side of mine, just holding me, his strength touching over my past, his firm soft fingers on my spine and somehow removing that madly crumpled shirt at the same time.

The flesh finally touching, the anticipation shortening my senses and the excitement of something rising through me that I want to feel over and over again, on a continuous loop.

And even when it was all over, it wasn't. The holding on to each other because that moment may not be reproduced and because it is too valuable to lose. Although afterwards, it was a long time before we could face each other.

TUCKED UP

The next day, waking up in my own grounded-to-my-shape bed, a fake and hideously patterned designer blanket, re-gifted from Susie after one of her many house and colour redesigns over the ages, which was giving the effect of tucking me in, I felt absurdly disappointed at first (and later) to be waking up on my own; I get a call from Daniella.
An urgent fancy coffee and catch-up was required she said.
She shook me into meeting her an hour later at the rather Boho vegan coffee shop that she had originally wanted to name *The Molly House*, in deference to all of the closeted older men at her gym who had stayed within the harsh boundaries of normality, and with their sad, unknowing wives who had certainly deserved better. Instead, she called this the *Boho Coffee Shop*, (as using the word vegan puts off the non-vegans and hence could result in loss of income – my ideas, always given freely).
This dining experience was tastefully decked out with mainly lavender-shaded crockery, and once mass-produced old sepia photographs of original ethic bean growers. Most of the men were half naked to suit all tastes, and the goats were fully in the buff, perhaps to suit some others. The original coffee pioneers. This coffee shop was only recently opened next to CP Fitness, (she has diversified in more way than one) as she'd been giving away too many free drinks at the gym. My idea, freely given, yet again.

Daniella, as per her usual 'I am always in control manner', had already ordered for me.

A soya latte, single shot, extra hot (like me, she said this every time, though I doubt I've ever heard that from anyone else) no chocolate, as who would ever think that chocolate powder on coffee was acceptable, she always said. Well, apart from me. She had also determined that I needed a warm butter-free croissant, and that was wrapped in a white napkin next to a pot of artisan plum and ginger jam, no spread.

It is very hard work being friends with a strong and authoritative vegan. Even a 'normal' vegan has its challenges.

She was dressed in the most fabulous pink and orange floral dress, totally as bonkers as William Morris, at his most insane, but in a supremely authentic way. The skirt was full and wide, the sleeves showing off very honed arms and with matching, pinkish, floral Cowboy boots, having just come back from the very wild west of America, she certainly could rock any look. Today please visualise Shania Twain blended with Beyonce. That don't impress me much single ladies.

'Oh my giddy aunt! You slept with him again', she opened with, eyes wide.

'Any good this time?' And then her expression altered a little, either sad for me or happy. She has this way of sucking you in with her tiny head movements. A tilt to her left, your right, means 'talk to me', the other way round is letting you see that she is listening, but you have got some serious thinking to do.

164

With me, it was a minuscule head-shake. No-one else would have seen this, so when she confirmed that I'd fallen, perhaps only physically (who would know?) perhaps I even cared, but there definitely had been a sea-change.

She said: 'Holly', tiny head shake. 'My lovely little Holly, you are so totally going to hate me.'

Long ago, in another dimension and within minutes of the Will reading, whilst still reeling, I had tasked Daniella to find out what dirt there may have been on Jonathan, ultimately forewarned is forearmed, and she had taken this project very seriously.

After becoming the unseen go-between between Susie's widower and me, it later turned out that she had also become his confidant.

The listening skills she had honed from her time on the ground in the war zones, stockpiling the *Elder's* from-the-ground gossip to be fed back to the Intelligence teams, and coupled with her inherent natural innocence caused people to fall into a kind of infatuation with her and they told her their deepest secrets.

They shared their past losses and their sense of failures, and with every story told, she helped them lighten their pain. She wrapped their sadness into soft bundles and stored them away, never opening them back up again for cheap gossip, or to use as a comparison to her own experiences, when she herself needed comfort.

Today though, the bundle she was about to open to me was more frightening than the lovechild of the Shania and Beyonce dress and ensemble she was wearing.

'I got to meet up with an old *Intelligence* friend when I was in Washington, thought I'd take the chance to see what he was up to now he's retired after a stint working with the Bureau, and we had a few *Jack's* for old times' sake.'

She was talking, and I somehow knew that I had already lost the fight that hadn't been mine to begin with.

'I don't know how to tell you Holly, he was so big and strong when he was younger, we almost had a thing' (who is she talking about?). 'And then I happened to mention you, and your big deal, and I said about the forensic podiatrist, and he remembered a guy some years ago who discovered the kid at the crime scene was a relative.'

While Daniella carried on talking, something rattled way deep in my subconscious, hidden underneath the snippets of useless information I carried, lost in a conversation fully fermented with the cheap wine that Susie used to force me to drink, about a case Jonathan had worked on just before they met and how once he had mentioned a sister, from a liaison his mother had with another man before she married his father and how the Catholic nuns cruelly left her with no option but to put the little girl up for adoption, virtually dragging the baby from womb to worthier parents.

'No lie, Holly' said Daniella, 'he covered it up and the guy is on death row!'

NEWS UPDATE

The body found in the stolen van outside the infamous primary school has been identified and the police have confirmed this is now being treated as murder.

THE THERAPIST, ENEMIES

By now, Dr Palmer had made some bold and life-
defying sweeping changes in her life. She knew her
fake facade was crumbling. The detached five bed-
roomed house (with much scope to modernise) had
once belonged to her parents and was passed to her
mortgage-free upon her father's death. As a result,
the partially listed building, dating back to the 1800s,
was, at present, worth a tidy sum.
It had a 'for sale' sign attached to the Flemish-bond-
brick wall that surrounded two thirds of the property.
That had been fixed firmly to the west side, as this
was the most effective position, the estate agent had
explained in a somewhat condescending manner
that appears requisite for that chosen career.
The lush green lawn was mowed in tidy rows and
the sharp sand (recommended by the slightly
grumpy but handsome enough gardener with whom
she had attempted to test her very rusty flirting skills
with earlier that year) had been spread over the
surface to prevent moss; or to help with the new
growth in the spring season, she hadn't really been
listening, she was the one doing the teasing.
The large gravelled drive up to the front door was
packed either side with an overabundance of roses
and magnolia, hydrangea and fuchsia.
All planted many years ago to provide colour
throughout the many changing seasons.
When the leaves dropped from those, they were
gathered into the appropriate mulch patches, and
then the red and oranges of the dogwoods and
chokeberry, the clashing autumnal shrubs, fell into
favour.

To anyone else this would have been the dream home. But Harriet's failed marriage and adoption of a large Gambian child, and his mother, coupled with a fake career and love of wine, had destroyed any chance of joy for her.

Going into the loft space all that time ago had started the fall and decline of this once-noble lady. The rest, as they say, was history.

All traces of both dead bodies long removed from her house.

The shadows they left behind were being replaced with daylight, with fresh air from open windows and the many lavender reed diffusers, plus the fabulous new matching pure soy paraben-free candles, from *Wick of Water Orton*, a place that Holly had highly recommended as she did their accounts too.

(More customers, more likely to keep the contract, more money for Holly; a no brainer really.)

This was a real treat. No more purposeful pound-shop poisoning for Bill Haley's stink. And added to this, and perhaps more importantly to her spiritual well-being, there was no critical cacophony, from feline or human.

The stairs to the loft space (scope to modernise) had been made safer with the addition of an antique wooden handrail from the local reclamation yard. The doctor suspected she knew of the reason the old lady had gone up there on that fateful day, but put that back into the recesses of her mind for now. She figured the handrail was in keeping with the rest of the house.

Bad taste. And that would make a nice selling point.

All of the old, and previously referenced as vintage, curtains, complete with fraying and naturally flaxen linings, along with the yellowing nets, had been replaced with a myriad of material from the local rag markets.

She enjoyed that shopping excursion. The fabric she had hand-sewn together, with many thumb pricks adding blood to the many vibrant colours which were already battling for independence.

More interestingly, there wasn't a hint of yellow cowardice in any of them.

A number of bonfires, at least one per week, without any complaints from the not-so-near neighbours, rid her of the old drapes and dusty memories.

She had smiled sadly as she recalled Manlafi quoting a finer man: 'either the curtains go, or I do'. He wasn't ever original.

Some books she kept, as burning reading matter was totally out of order. That behaviour belonged to other types of monsters.

The love stories that her old friend and combatant used to read and reread had been divided equally between the three local charity shops.

Probably on the way from those to the tip, to be burnt, so page-turned and decorated with Kaddy's spit and pink lipstick, and Bill Haley's neat arse-stamps visible for eternity, fixed firmly with vomited fur balls.

Possibly more tellingly, her sad old once-white dressing gown, coveted by her husband all that time ago, had been donated to the recycling fabric charity, perhaps to fund more terrorists on the other side of the wars that the West loved to start.

She used the bins in the supermarket carpark – to hide the embarrassing evidence, and a new green replacement, a kimono style wrap, complete with dancing dragons, was purchased, online obviously and two sizes bigger than she thought she was; a known trick to make ladies feel slim. It didn't work for her.

Dr Harry had arranged with the local council to take the old refrigerator, complete with non-PC chlorofluorocarbons to the local dumping ground and treated herself to a fabulous turquoise American one, which even made ice, just in case she couldn't be bothered to re-chill the wine.

Her nightly drinking had remained the same, but she could justify this to herself if she ever felt she needed to. And anyway, she was confident that she used alcohol for pleasure and not dependency (cannot get addicted to alcohol allegedly).

She had recently proofread an article on this very subject matter for an old alcoholic colleague from her general practitioner days, who was looking to publish these findings (not research), and justify his own id/ego reliance. No objective research offered. And none taken.

Another sweeping change was to take on a new client. And against her better judgement too, as she knew of this person from both Holly and Susie's sessions.

Whilst objectively and professionally she knew she ought not to, but as the mid-life crisis took hold, and with her thoughts about retirement becoming ever-present, she really did want to meet this third wheel, if only to pin it all together and finish that chapter once and for all.

And Daniella Ingle did not disappoint. Within a few seconds of meeting this fabulous and elegant creation, Dr Harry felt herself fluff both sides of her wilted hair and want to reapply her chapped orange lipstick. Daniella did this to people.
They either wanted to be her or they fall in love with her. Both worked for Daniella.
It turned out that Harriet's mother-in-law, known for her vicious tongue, was about to spill the beans on an old colleague of her son. As we are now aware, the ruthless manipulator was motivated, cunning and destined from an early age to be a success, and had left many children scattered in his wake. And more proof was needed for Holly to finally get what was due to her.
Having survived many therapists during her meta morphosis, and plenty more afterwards, Daniella didn't need the fifty-something flabby and fraudulent psychotherapist with the extremely bad taste in soft furnishing and antique tat, for any mental health issues.
She certainly didn't need to see the previous competition (after all, it was Daniella that Manny wanted to spend the rest of his life with. His words). No. She was going to use this washed-out confidence trickster to find some evidence on Iain Hastings. Anything to help Holly get her long overdue and well-deserved pay-out.
The old woman, Kaddy Sarr, obviously had something hidden in the house, the loft perhaps, as the stairs to it was where she had fallen over and squished the life out of Bill Haley. Daniella had to get access to it.

The thing about being a fitness instructor who was a trained killer and who excelled in negotiating with terrorists, is that you can say things like 'I'm not a player, I'm the coach' and people love it.

They feel that you've let them into your deepest secrets, that you're not a manipulator, hey, but look at you! You're just a regular fun person.

Daniella was usually very confident in getting the most out of anyone, except perhaps Holly, and that was an ongoing work in progress.

With Dr Harry, Daniella knew she had to let her feel she was in control and that she could help, with whatever ailment Daniella could manifest after her initial summing up.

'Developing friendships' is what she offered for starters. Now Dr Harry wasn't anyone's fool, for she had caught the glimpse of wheels turning when she asked how she could help.

For once, Daniella had left a slight gap before answering.

Maybe to show she didn't know how to start, but hopefully she had left enough of a trap for Dr Harry to fall into.

WHEN IRISH EYES STOPPED SMILING

Daniella hadn't 'accidentally' run into anyone in America, of course she hadn't. This was a trip that had been planned with her usual and absolute finite detail. She'd won the confidence of Jonathan over a number of months, and with a letter of introduction in her vast vegan-leather effect purse, and a promise from Jonathan that he would call his sister as soon as he would, please, and arrange a meeting, Daniella set about looking up her old US contacts with a view to fulfilling her earlier promise to Holly. That of finding anything on Jonathan.

The sister had been renamed Carla. His mother had wanted to christen her May Kathleen, but the baby was taken away from her within half an hour of her arrival in this cruel world and the adoption papers signed by a responsible adult, as there was no way that Kathleen May Egan was considered responsible for anything, having fallen from grace and letting her whole family down in the process.

Carla had stayed in the house where her daughter, and Jonathan's niece, had been brutally attacked and left for dead.

A one-time nice but now grey residential area, where a Philip Larkin dog may have added some much-needed flea cheer to the inhabitants, Carla greeted this very strange English lady at the door to her tiny house and invited her in for the American version of tea, no milk but powder.

The English lady had brought someone with her that Carla thought she recognised from the ordeal that had torn her beating heart from her tortured soul those few years ago, replacing it with an emptiness so utterly painful that it was the only thing that had kept the semblance of her being alive.

She wouldn't remember much from the hour-long conversation, though she visibly lightened, albeit briefly, when she heard that Daniella was a very good friend of her brother, as this helped her to validate that she had once belonged to something, someone, anyone. This too-late knowledge brought no real relief.

After all those years with her new American-Irish family, being told she should count herself 'real lucky lady, that anyone would want to adopt her', she would look out over the backyard every night and pray to the dying stars that there was a family some-where who had just forgotten to collect her, and that they would come and rescue her very soon.

But they never came. Later, she shacked up with and then married a wastrel. She had really tried hard to love him, like they made so easy in the movies, but this wasn't Hollywood, and she had never been taught how to love. Carla had his child, felt something for that child, which may have been an inherent Irish tenderness, but lost that child when the good-for-nothing, having already killed many times before, came back late one night, barefooted, broke, ready for a fight, and attempted to kidnap his own daughter.

When Daniella and her ex-FBI friend left, after revisiting and photographing the girl's dusty and air-locked bedroom long after the murder had taken place, and where the cheap Walmart duvet-cover faded in stripes where the sun had once crept through the ancient paper-thin curtains, Carla returned to the scene of her crime.

The pain still hung in the room and permeated from the old wallpaper peeling from the dampness of so many tears.

This space had been locked since the scenes of crimes officers, the FBI representatives, working with Jonathan, and the local *LEO's* had trampled over every inch, looking for evidence, for motive, for opportunity. Every mans' hearts were heavy, broken at the evil men can do.

And now Carla just sat on her child's bed. She held the worn-out and faded, tomato-ketchup coloured teddy bear that her daughter had tried to protect herself with, close to her own face and she hoped she could still smell the talcum powder loveliness of her little, unloved girl.

She had realised that this latest visit could now expose what actually happened back then. It's all too late, she thought.

Carla, perhaps finally at peace with herself, calmly pulled the trigger of the same pistol that she should have used on her husband that night, straight through the roof of her mouth.

As everyone knows, it's usually the person closest to the victim that is responsible.

Daniella, of course, didn't know this at the time, as she was overly enthused with the evidence that had always been available, but subtly not re-reviewed. Her friend had managed to keep unsanctioned copies of all the files he ever had worked on, as he said that one day he may write his biography, and would use these as references. On the journey back to his ranch, which made Daniella giggle every time she said that out loud, they were completely unaware of the chain of events they had started, or the tail that had been with them since her arrival into Washington-Reagan National Airport.

The old pals and once almost-lovers picked up some cans of *Budweiser*, a litre of *Jack Daniels* and a huge block of ice, and braced themselves for a good long night of fact-hunting. Which was often easier to do than say.

The ex-FBI officer had always had a soft spot for Daniella, even more so when she was Dan, but the law enforcers of the Western world can't show any weaknesses, exploitation isn't reserved just for the rich and famous, and for our lawman, and law-women to be gay would mean contempt; and if he was still working then he would, most certainly, have lost his job.

He recalled his mother's sad deathbed tale of being forced to go through conversion therapy when she lost her early career prospects with the American civil service as part of the *Lavender scare*.

It must have worked. She married his dad, had him, and never smiled again.

Lavender. Purity, grace and silence.

With the tragic memory of his mother's sadness, he realised that if he gave in to fancying the real Daniella, his self-esteem and newly discovered sense of self-worth could be torn to shreds.

Fortunately, Daniella was less attractive as a woman to him (even the most accepting Americans have deep-South prejudices, he would have said, defending his quest for acceptable normality), so instead, this way, he could spend more time with her and feel no qualms about helping with the exposure of this case.

Even if it was technically against the laws of his land. What would not be accepted though, was that any new or contradicting evidence, if found, could be admitted in a re-trial to sway a new judge or jury. This perpetrator had confessed to many similar child abductions and killings, he needed to be locked up, and stay locked up, until his death. No matter how many times he swore he hadn't killed his daughter. While all the gut instincts and obvious facts pointed to this man having indeed killed Jonathan's niece, the one piece of evidence 'found' at the scene to prove his guilt was taken from the perps lodging house, the boot had been hastily extracted and planted accordingly. This was then positioned in the child's bedroom with the law enforcement officer's fingerprints wiped from the outer fabric, the many footprints inside the house proving that our guy was there at the scene (he was, as he used to live there) and therefore was the killer (he wasn't) and the forensic evidence doesn't lie. He was still going to hang by the neck until he was dead. And so he should.

Maybe if it was later in his career, and if the child hadn't been a relative, and the pain from his marriage wasn't so overwhelming, Jonathan would have found genuine evidence to link the killer to the crime.

But, as the case is closed, the right man on death row, and with only his surviving wife as a witness, the ends, this time, could justify the means.

The constant judgemental weight of hindsight would wear this man down.

THE FADING THERAPIST AND HOLLY

Holly was early to what she was planning to be her very last session with Dr Harry. Holly was usually early for every appointment, but having downsized with another client, perhaps as a result of Dr Harry letting *Mop, Shop and Crop*, Housekeepers for the Discerning, go, after her mother-in-law died, and instead directly employing the gardener they had provided as part of the *Crop*, (cash in hand) and therefore cutting out the middleman, the non-financial expert patronisingly explained to Holly. She was completely unaware of the trickle-down economic effect, as she was with most things outside of her psychology magazines, *YouTube* Gurus and how-to-dress-successfully guidance. As a consequence of losing yet another client, *Mop, Shop and Crop* had to make further cutbacks and they now only needed Holly for the year-end accounts and monthly VAT and payroll, hence she had completed that task, mailing the payslips and the quarterly accounts to be signed off, from the local Post Office. Thank goodness for the marketing guru who ran the candle makers, Holly thought. Taking advantage of the promise of the early spring weather, she had ditched her car in the village and had walked the half a mile journey through the freshly mown and churned up dog walking and dogging park, where she was approached by a stout lady in an ancient red-felt hat, who asked her if she had lost her dog.

'About two years ago' said Holly mischievously, but it had fallen on deaf ears, and so she carried on regardless to Dr Harry's for her weekly debate, as a consultation had been pointless for a very long time. Seeing Daniella leave the old-fashioned Victorian detached house, recently having survived some sort of makeover, the house not Daniella, had thrown Holly. Holly had shared stories with Daniella about Dr Harry, and while Daniella had laughed about the way Harry operated, she had never once shown any further interest, certainly not in being treated in any way.

Holly stayed rooted to her wet patch, her feet sinking further into the mud, trying to recall the last conversation with Daniella with reference to the Jonathan dirt gathering task. She knew she had said not to bother anymore with the digging, as she would face whatever the big secret was, maybe she already knew. And because she no longer saw Jonathan as the opposition, he was just Susie's last successful conquest. And as well, whatever he may have on Holly wasn't really worth the paper being wasted.

When the coast was suitably clear, she watched the still streaked stained glass door from her vantage point for a long time before approaching, telling herself that if Harriet had kept the discerning housekeepers on, she'd be able to see though it, spot anyone hiding in the garden and the cleanliness would make a better impression for any potential buyers.

But still Holly couldn't help feeling the shadow of something past wrapping itself around her, filling her with that dread of memories from slamming doors and breath held while waiting for the footsteps to go in another direction, away from her.

Holly may have been the meek, quiet one, but that was as a result of her husband. Before then she had a natural killer analyst-mind, a sarcastic tongue, she was an empath, and she saw patterns long before the other guys did.

She was getting stronger; she was regaining her confidence in her abilities and herself, and she knew where Iain's embezzlements were hidden.

Admittedly, she thought to herself, and in fairness to Daniella, she had originally tasked her with finding something on Jonathan, but that was before, and now, it didn't seem so important after all.

Holly was sure she had stressed this to Daniella. So was this linked to Harriet Palmer to Kaddy Sarr?

Holly had once sorted Kaddy back-log of late accounts out, to stop her from going to jail, she threatened. This trawling through old paperwork had shown some interesting places of work from her time back in London.

Kaddy had kept her little tokens coveted from many offices and houses, all labelled neatly as though waiting to be presented with great fanfare, should they be required.

Holly found Manny's birth certificate, father unknown, but Kaddy had scribbled something on it.

With this vital record there was a great deal of correspondence from when Kaddy had left the Stock Broker's offices down south all of those years ago.

Of course Holly had scanned through them.

Irrelevant to her task in-hand, that of getting Kaddy to pay some tax, but enough for this former anti-money laundering investigator to remove anything that may either prove useful or later bite her in the arse. Holly's arse of course, not Kaddy's.

Having hesitated for long enough, her feet were freezing, and making sure she delayed further by stopping to scrape the mud from her shoes on the gravel and to sniff every early flower and bud on the way to the main door, where she paused for a while again.

Hopeful that more than enough time had elapsed to ensure no-one would think she had just missed Daniella, she rang the doorbell and waited for the charlatan to answer the door, one last time, she said to herself.

Her father would have said: 'Take the time to smell those roses, Holly'.

JONATHAN, BEFORE SUSIE

Before the flight to the ill-fated discovery of his
sibling which resulted in the actions he would later
regret deeply, and while waiting in the bright though
drab security area, having been asked to 'please
step aside sir', Jonathan hadn't had access to his
mobile phone. This, along with his medical case,
was being assessed for potential weaponry before
any further embarkation could occur.
His name had pinged on that invisible, to others,
radar, and the border guards were obviously
concerned about who they let out of the country
these days.
Jonathan was waiting on a call that may have
changed his future, but when it never came, he
didn't know he hadn't missed it.
Still in the relatively early years of feet-policing, it
hadn't become any easier to explain what a forensic
podiatrist is. Jonathan had heard every attempt at
humour, every foot joke and never laughing at them
the third or twentieth time, in any language.
Although he was on his way over to America where
the Federal Bureau of Investigation's tools would be
available to him, more updated of course, with all the
latest artificial intelligence software, more AI
chemical-sniffing false-dogs and all the data for
every single associated crime ordered, organised,
accounted for and ready for his arrival, Jonathan still
liked to take some of his own familiar tricks of the
trade. His security blanket, if you like.
This bag of goodies was what was interesting the
Customs boys now.

Having been asked to open his medical case, such as it was, they made a show of snapping on a new pair of latex gloves per item.

'And what would this be used for sir?', snap.

'These are simply stronger lenses for my strap-on binoculars' said Jonathan.

'Strap on', snap, snap, to the amusement of the other ten-year-old colleague trapped inside the uniform of a power-mad older child, who also made a show of snapping on his own tricks of the trade. The blue, rubber and multi-purpose gloves.

Wearily, as Jonathan hadn't yet learned to not use that expression, or maybe in spite of hearing it so many times, he attempted to explain why leaving the hands free when investigating crime scenes was more sensible; that if you were fiddling with your kit constantly then you couldn't ensure that you were paying enough courtesy to the victim. But of course, the officers had collapsed at 'fiddling with your kit' and didn't bother listening to Jonathan much at all after that. These would make great dinner party stories if either of them was invited to such things. They weren't.

Normally this unnecessary obstruction would have caused Jonathan to suffer some mild anxiety at the thought of missing his plane, or worse, being the last to get on, even though on this occasion he would be turning left when he boarded, courtesy of the FBI, he had never been one for attention. This time though, having recently discovered that his wife hadn't really cared for him at all, and was still sleeping with her 'one true love', he was experiencing the bewildering hollowness of betrayal.

Not even into the first full year of marriage, after spending a fortune for the wedding which she was had always dreamt of. At the fairy-tale, and hopefully haunted, Irish Castle, the hotel staff's children, mostly Polish, represented the Little People and the leprechauns.

The magic of the thousands of glittering and swaying solar-powered fairy lights flickering for their evening service, hung over the many weathered fruit trees in the magnificent, once formal gardens. Their short honeymoon was in the only restored wing in a remote part of the castle, where the powerful Irish Sea would carry its music through the open windows, which even when they were closed still blew a gale.

It would appear that Jonathan wasn't in fact a storybook prince after all. He may have looked like every woman's secret fantasy Heathcliff, the detachment his first wife had mistaken for broody passion.

Her personification of Jonathan had left him temporarily confused about his actual identity, and by trying afterwards to become her illusion just to keep her loving him, he had failed. Heathcliff hadn't broken her heart, she had broken it, and in breaking it she broken his.

When Jonathan finally boarded the flight to Dulles Airport in Washington, as he had feared, the last to board, to the derisive whooping and cackling from the passengers in the cheaper seats, he had the divorce papers still, unopened, but not his mobile phone. Both, it could appear later, may have distracted him.

THE NERVOUS THERAPIST AND HOLLY

Dr Harry knew she had little time left in which she could continue in the role of anyone's therapist. Boundaries had long been crossed and although she hoped that no-one in authority would get to hear of them, in her heart, in the little bit of professionalism she clung on to, she understood she had broken every code.

The recent visit from Daniella had confirmed she was clinging to wet paper straws.

Seeing Holly today would have to be the time to break the news that she was leaving the area.

The house was sold, the grass over Bill Haley's grave was growing back, although a shade of green much darker that the rest of the lawn, something to do with how deep the grave was, the *Crop* man had tried to explained. No, today she had to tell Holly that she could recommend another therapist, but really didn't think Holly needed any kind of head-therapy. Maybe a yoga session or some healing crystals or perhaps a Tibetan-bowl sound-immersion course. Any one of those would work for that sweet little naive soul.

Holly hadn't brought up the subject of seeing Daniella on her last visit, patient confidentiality or her usual general cowardice or something, but she definitely had noticed a change in Dr Harry.

Today though, using her 'pull yourself together and face the world' camouflage, that she had been working on since childhood, she really had wanted to lash out.

Holly rang the antiquated bell and the door was opened immediately.

And as much as she had wanted to say: 'Why did Daniella come here, is it because she's sleeping your husband?' She didn't.

What she actually said was 'Daniella said she enjoyed her session with you, she's so looking forward to seeing you again.' Two can play any game.

Dr Harry hadn't expected this so soon. She knew of Holly's new confidence spurt, much like babies when they hit the six-ounce feeds and grow before your eyes, this child was growing and regaining herself, things laid to waste in the wilder-years rediscovered and polished.

But seriously, so soon? Was it really all down to decent sex?

Harriet welcomed Holly into the newly refurbished living room that had been painted with a touch of fresh emulsion, sailor-white with blue undertones over the existing old and fetid wood-chip wallpaper. A new teapot, the antique tea-cosy (please, God, no) some matching mugs, her rules all shaken up as these were already laid out on huge tray, Harry had said it had been a pleasure to meet with her friend Daniella. And how utterly gorgeous she was, and how very kind she had been. About Kaddy and Bill Haley, that was.

Knowing this was crap, but desperate to find out what Holly knew of the game-playing, without asking directly, and having honed no further skills, because Harriet as we know, had always known better. Instead, she opted for the silent approach in the vain hope that Holly would fill in some of the gaps.

187

Holly took the cheap and flawed mug from her hostess and asked her how she was faring without the mad couple.

For a moment, Harriet thought she was referring to her ex-husband Manlafi and his new love, Daniella – yes, of course she knew, Manny wouldn't let something like that go by unannounced – but seeing the absolute joy on his face to be 'so in love', and 'oh, the magnificent sex' was enough to stir the acid from the previous evening's warm wine right into the heart of her sad uselessness.

Although she had managed to say to Daniella 'good luck in your new bed', as she was leaving. Under her breath.

'Kitty cat, Harry, and Kaddy?' Said Holly, enjoying the confusion this had caused.

And Dr Harry, manoeuvred as the smarter person had fully intended, indeed proceeded to project all of her emotions away from Manny to Kaddy, to satisfy at least one part of the equation, and in doing so, the doctor became the patient, and it felt so good.

Knowledge is power, according to Sir Francis Bacon. *Scientia est potentia* Holly.

And with that, she walked away from Dr Harriet Palmer for good.

KADDY SARR, HA HA HA

Kaddy Sarr may have been the mother-in-law from hell, but, in her defence, her life hadn't brought the best out of her. With a child outside of wedlock, herself a child outside of wedlock, brought up by a cousin, or an auntie, who may or may not have been a blood relative, she was fed on either Benachin or Domoda, wearing a different fataro clothing style weekly (but not on Sundays), Kaddy's natural Gambian culture and strengths relied on hearsay and random words, watered down by too much time in the fragmented and soulless West.

As was typical of these expectations, from both sides of the spectrum, Kaddy fell into the invisible world of night-time cleaners. Another auntie to help out with baby Manlafi (whose name meant 'didn't want') during the twilight shifts, so many houses and offices to clean – dependant on where the 'agency' sent her.

Kaddy was a good cleaner and a reliable worker and word soon got around. 'Please can we have the *jolly black girl*' became her own conceited mantra when she was given more hours and the better positions, no more shitty lavatories or stairwells, but the fancier offices instead.

When she moved away from London (too many illegals she said) to the West Midlands where the majority of her 'family' had already relocated, she naturally fell into a leadership role, and rather than be the jolly black girl she started her own cleaning agency, *Jolly Cleaners*, using the local immigrants, and quickly developed a rather impressive company.

189

Not on the books you understand, (before she met Holly) but that meant no minimum wages and so she could undercut most other tenders and also claim some benefits that, had her own taxes been collected in her earlier career, would have been deemed acceptable.

Kaddy and Manny lived, for a long time, in a mostly white area on the outskirts of Birmingham where she would park her sign-written van over the neighbours illegally dropped kerb – in her mind, if the council hadn't given planning permission then it didn't count – some rules needed adhering to.

Manny went to a very fancy school following his shambolic junior education. He had attended a hideously biased and typically non-inclusive inner-city school, where his was the only mixed-race face. Little variegation there.

After winning a scholarship and the financial support of Birmingham City Council, diversity was the new shibboleth for this troubled governmental division, Kaddy would drop him right outside his swanky secondary school (on the double yellow lines much to the exasperation of the other parents and, indeed, the weekly letters from the headmaster himself) with a daily reminder of 'we are good enough'.

His mother's mantra became Manny's: 'I am good enough'.

And whilst everyone could try this sacred utterance on for size, the actual words, as they so often do, took on a more menacing acceptance for Manlafi Sarr. *I am good enough* meant he was better than anyone else.

So Hum.

Manny loved to dress up in his mother's idea of her native clothing and had worked his way through her wardrobe more than once.

He would try on her huge lacy bras (stuffed with his colourful organic bamboo socks, only the best for him, he said). He would match this look with her enormous gossamer pants, pinned on one side with a pretty, though mostly toothless, hair clip; taking advantage of this fancy dressing up every time his mother was out at work. Or at the doctors. She was there a lot.

He would twirl around the house and the garden, sometimes adding one of her many chaotic wigs and serene religious head coverings throughout all of his developing years. He took plenty of her underwear with him when going on to his further formal education, through the two non-diverse top universities. The *Dreaming Spires* for Law and the other one just for the hell of it. Manny was obsessed with his own body (his enormous tackle).

In his youth he was transfixed with his mother's body (only got a good glimpse just the once, and that was closely followed with a proper Gambian-style maternal beating).

He was enraptured with the bodies of his school friends, all sexes. At junior school they stripped off in the woods for a dare and at senior school they could share a shower. At both universities there was so much free and easy sex. Every vintage for every taste. Such love, such freedom, such joy!

He loved bodies, he told everyone.

And as Manny successfully flew through the education systems and became a professional man, his depraved and distorted love of master-and-slave sex had to be contained to foreign trips, where it was seemingly more acceptable to love bodies in this way. Especially those of small children.

Kaddy was Dr Harriet's first Gambian patient at the GP surgery, and her most regular. Although the *Primum non nocere* approach went right out of the window, as this obviously very heathy woman was just so utterly stubborn, the patient was insistent on seeing this doctor at least weekly. Her OCD tendencies of which she was very proud (these included cleaning the consultation chair with half a packet of antiseptic wipes every time, revisiting the door three times to ensure no-one could hear, and pulling the sleeves down over her wrists four times each) weren't really a reason for the visit. What she needed, and ultimately wore Dr Palmer into, was a home visit.

During this visit, after meticulously ensuring that not only Manny stayed at home, dressing in his own clothes and performing at his most alluring, Kaddy managed to leave the two of them alone, having already told her son that he must marry a lady, a professional lady. Not for any grandchildren, or to further his career, but to make him normal again. Every mother always knows what is best for her unwanted child.

The alone time was a huge success as a dinner date was made and kept, Harriet doing the driving to ensure she didn't drink, and Manny accepting Harriet picking up the bill too. All part of the great seduction, sucker. And boy, did she fall for it.

DANIELLA FAILS

Daniella Ingle had experienced a lot of things.
She was born in the wrong body to the wrong father,
in Yorkshire to make matters worse, and as a result
had managed to rid herself of most the idioms that
made her native folk so ridiculed, yet admired.
She certainly could have used some of them now.
She ought to have been more direct with Harriet,
without breaking any confidences, after all, the good
doctor would surely have known that Holly had some
dirt on Susie, hence the ridiculous Will. She could
have said 'by 'eck Harry, we need to get t'bottom of
this' and Harriet would see the sense and offer help,
as most people love the bluntness of the Yorkshire
folk. According to Yorkshire folklore.
But it just wasn't in this tyke. It, the sham Yorkshire
bravado, had been slowly seeping away as her new
life was being built. A bit like that dam. Filling up with
the new stuff, after dredging away the mud, weeds
and other rubbish.
Daniella's own sacred utterance had been that she
unfailingly knew better, in every situation. Which had
appeared true enough, until now. She was clinging
onto the many layers she had wrapped herself in.
Uncertainty was still at her core, but now the
darkness was rising, again.
Dr Harriet Palmer, who had always gone by her
maiden name as she must have known Manny Sarr
was too fine a catch to keep so hadn't bothered
changing it, had suspected that Daniella had ulterior
motives. She certainly didn't need Harriet's type of
therapy.

And even though the doctor would admit to not being that great a counsellor, she was of a certain age where she had seen and experienced more than she would have wanted. With the gut instincts of a thousand generations past, she knew where her husband's secrets were hidden, and how much damage they could do to them both. She also suspected who may be after them. Many night-time visits to the loft after her much-younger husband had left, discovering his, and others, secret legacies. Stomach turning recordings for twisted audiophiles. And much evidence of blackmail. Evidence of torture and pain. Evidence that would have broken anyone else. But not this woman.

When people don't talk truthfully, when their words get distorted along the way, as how they are given to how they are received can cross over many interpretations, then every conversation becomes a minefield, and the chances of getting out of mine-fields with limbs intact become far fewer the further down the rabbit hole of deceit one decides to travel. So, Daniella was now at a loss. The 'friendship' line she had opened with at her first encounter with Dr Harry wasn't really a complete lie, but it wasn't the whole truth.

The friend she was referring to may not have actually been identified openly at that stage, supposition only, but she now understood she had dismissed her opponent's ability to see through her shit. Daniella Ingle, with all her experience of spitting ISIS leaders and Yorkshire bigotry, was losing her edge in this battle. And she knew it.

Love does that to you.

In her desperate attempt to fulfil the early mission she had chosen to accept from Holly, that of finding out anything – anything at all, getting any dirt on either Susie or Jonathan, she had lost her own sense of impartiality. Falling in lust and then love with Dr Harry's rather gorgeous husband, although his weirdness was beginning to seep out of his strange pores and into hers, Daniella's head was more than a little messed up.

And although Holly may have since said, more than once, that she didn't care about the dirt anymore, Daniella had persisted in this sorry plight. For some reason known only to herself. If she could only understand that part now. Love had done that to her.

Harriet, on the other hand, knew of Manlafi's weirdnesses very early on in their marriage.

More than once (a day) she had seen him wearing her clothes, most notably the (then new) dressing gown, naked underneath with his huge limp dick on show most of the time, taunting her, she had once hoped.

She watched him pottering around in the orchard area at the far end of the garden where the new shoots from the *Greasy Pippin* apples that Susie had given her two summers ago, competed for the sun's blessings along with the other trees.

The fruit never eaten, it was left to rot in the living room; the one that was as out of date as the rest of her house, the one with the dead and dusty hyacinths.

The room in which both Susie and Holly had marvelled at Dr Harry's attempt to show them what she thought she knew. The wedding video to Manlafi Sarr. Both the video and the room had carried a sense of sadness, the hints went unacknowledged by both of her clients. Another great weight of failure. All seriously contending for group wrist-slitting.

The *Greasy Pippin* remains, on the other hand, had been nurtured by the other shrubbery and the clever fruit trees, after compost was spread over the many flower beds, and they shared the warmed autumn floors, year in and year out, reseeding themselves many times over the hallowed ground; the blind soil beasts solemnly moving these sacred pips to fresh and fertile pastures new, and the bees gladly sharing their other pollens and DNA around their unique flight-paths home.

As Harriet thought of herself as a well-informed mental health worker, she had tolerated Manny's behaviour and it was never discussed. Neither did she mention the physical porn magazines (catering for all tastes, or lack of) those not hidden away too well in the loft, and she never asked why he didn't just use the internet like any 'normal' person – the irony was missed by herself.

She also never questioned the USB stick found by her old work computer, still attached to the television in the cold living room, the room that Manny had earmarked as theirs only and where they had done their pre-marriage smooching.

This inhospitable room was rarely used since.

This affection was in the early days of the marriage, so it seemed to Harriet that Manlafi had possibly left it there deliberately, to carry on destroying her. Although originally, she thought these were old patient's records that the six-year data protection rule dictated must be destroyed.

She inserted the stick and watched her last hope of his love leave her.

Instead of any transcripts, this lonely woman watched a grainy recording of her husband's dick being 'attended' by a myriad mixed bunch of sexes and ages, including, or so she thought she heard, one of his clients who was married to one of her patients.

Dr Harry, having been let down big time by her own husband and the failure of all her early princess dreams – becoming a doctor, marrying a handsome man, having children, living happily ever after, knew everything that she needed to know. She knew that Daniella had an axe of her own to grind.

You see people don't change. They can change their hair colour, their body shape, they can add boobs and bum-fillers – for goodness sake they can even change their biological sex, but they can't change the person who inherited the hair colour, their body shape, and the inherent behaviours of a hundred generations.

A lion will always be a lion. A fucking mess will always be a fucking mess.

Yes, we're talking about you, Dr Palmer. You knew early on, and yet you did not stop him.

IAIN SPILLS SOMETHING

Iain Hastings was rolling from one disaster to another tragic train-wreck. He was suffering a three-day-weekend hangover and his dependence on the hard-stuff that had once made him the biggest profits was now becoming more than a money-seeping habit.

His work routines were suffering greatly, no longer could he make the necessary excuses on behalf of the complex entity structures his team gave to him for the final approvals. Even if the ordinary folk can't follow the money trail, the financial sector uses the likes of Iain Hastings and his expertise to rubber-stamp the financial authorities' many fluid and loose requirements. Risk aversion or something. To assess and accept that the potential client's monies are clean. And if not clean at source, then definitely laundered by the time they are taken on as yet another risk to the banking institution of their choice. Banking has its own boxes to tick.

Itch's formally managed bluster and his once brilliant brain were in rapid decline. The people around him were suffering. He was suffering. He did not have the energy for casual encounters, as, and even more perturbing, he couldn't get it up at all these days. His early morning coffee had bits in, the sort the French liked to call dirty coffee. And if all of that wasn't enough to wear a person out, he'd had two missed calls and a voicemail suggesting an urgent breakfast invitation, from the second to last person he would ever want to share any time with. Ms Ingle.

You could imagine his desire at being seen out with this total freak of nature. But he caved in and called Daniella to arrange a quick chat to see if he could fob her off, as he was still suffering. More so when she refused to be fobbed off and instead determined the place to meet. Not the Boho coffee shop at her place but a well-known high-street chain, one of Hasting's clients, oddly enough from the shell company in Colombia that he still liaised with. Daniella appeared to have intentionally chosen this café as it was close enough to his workplace, and she could be certain someone would notice them together. And how could he have refused? His brain was frying but he hadn't got to where he was by not being intuitive. Perhaps she just wanted to meet up to talk about the divorce, the money settlement. She didn't.

'Iain, darling', she said with that wonderfully honed and mellifluous voice of hers. 'I'm in the process of renewing my Will and gather you know someone who can keep a secret?'

With all of his years of him acting the bully or being the player who always had the upper hand, he recognised a loaded question when he heard it. She knew, and he knew that she knew, that however he responded it would take the conversation in a direction that he had no intention of going in.

What this expert dealer in hope decided to do was to throw a curve ball straight back at Daniella.

He told her his Will changed with every peccadillo, and he even smiled then, a wonderful wide smile (perfect teeth) that caught her off-guard, albeit temporarily.

While on this charm-offensive he asked her what she had to leave and was she worth bumping off.

Iain Hastings didn't get to shaft commodity traders anymore. He didn't get to play with the high-fliers either as their acts had been totally cleaned up.

Or, at least, they were supposed to have been to satisfy the local financial conduct authorities. But old game-playing didn't die hard and he still had some innate and jaded streak of self-absorption. In this reconstructed moment, he was Bonaparte.

He thought that he should try and diffuse the situation and therefore went full pelt with his Waterloo. Daniella.

Unfortunately for him, Daniella had also played with bigger and taller bad boys. Dumped by her own parents, she had faced off the bigoted coal miners, proved the disgusted military personnel wrong, and had the Federal Bureau on her side for goodness sake. She was definitely not going to be blindsided by this pathetic excuse of a man.

She smiled sweetly back at him, threw her perfect three shades of blonde hair back over her shoulders and pushed her face so close he could not avoid her beautiful eyes, and happily felt a twinge in his underpants. 'It still works' was his fleeting thought. Then she said 'I am certainly worth bumping off, *Bitch*' watching his face twist when she bastardised his hated pet name. 'And I would like to know the name of your solicitor – the one that keeps all of the secrets, you know, the one that changes the Will with every marriage and child you have.'

Daniella sat back and observed the realisation washing over the once-handsome face of this broken combatant.

Realisation and something else – relief, perhaps. Had she made the rookie error of asking a question to which she hadn't known the answer? Daniella didn't want to go off track. She waited.

'What is it you really want?' Hastings had finally asked, as both he and Napoleon knew never to interrupt your enemy while they were making a mistake.

Daniella left his words hanging while she turned to the passing barista and ordered some more coffee. Not that she wanted any, but she had learned the rules of effective listening over the years. Give him something to distract himself. Make him feel he is gathering his strength and position again. Then she would destroy him.

'The truth, of course.'

Iain hadn't been spat on by the *Elders* in the Levant, he couldn't remember anyone spitting on him to be honest, but then he was fairly tall, and so Daniella spitting the word 'truth' out perturbed him for a number of reasons. The main one being, which truth was she after, and then, what version of it to give her, and to what gain and why now?

Hastings knew about her 'thing' with Manny, his close friend and non-solicitor, no recordings of any of their stuff yet, but he can wait. He knew Manny wouldn't have shared any pillow talk – too risky for him.

And if all of these things span neatly inside his head whilst he was forming his first sentence, his face didn't reflect anything, as he knew that history is a set of lies everyone finally agrees on. No-one would have been any the wiser.

He said: 'My son killed Susie.'

TOMMY CRACKS

Tommy missed his mum now more than ever before. He missed her abuse; he always knew where he was with that. He missed the noise from the televisions turned up so loudly that when she yelled at him, he genuinely didn't hear her. And still now, he won't.

He was so far down his own filthy drug-running catacombs that he simply didn't know how to climb out. He should never have been taking the stuff. Rule number one, dumbass.

He thought he was being so smart, setting up his own team. Recruiting the ten-and-eleven-year-olds, giving them the sharp blades and training them up, his way, after getting them hooked on weed and the huge money-earning potential, and then he had run into the lovely Daniella, literally, as the target education establishment he had last focused on was smack-bang next to her gym.

Unbeknownst to Tommy, Daniella had been watching out for the pushers and runners at the local school. She had been observing him and his actions and waiting for the perfect moment to casually engage with him.

With all of the experience from her time in the different sections of the military, she knew more than most people would ever want to know about the money trail of drugs and the systemic effects of that vile trade. The terrorism funding, the kidnapping, raping and torturing and the total devastation and destruction of the kids and those left behind.

Most parents have no clue what their offspring are up to on a daily basis, the liberals can say they value their children's freedom and lifestyle choices, and the non-liberals use their wisdom to stifle any creativity. Who would want to be a parent?

From the conversations Susie and Daniella had exchanged all those months ago, and those Daniella shared with Holly, they all knew Tommy was on the slow downward slope to jail.

She had asked Susie about his father's role in the upbringing, but again Susie deflected with a joke and a change of subject. Daniella really had found it so much easier dealing with the Afghani *Elders* than Susie Bennet.

Tommy wasn't Susie though. He hadn't had the chance to learn the art of manipulation or that of the victim, from her. He was a tall scared skinny kid with a very large nose which was already showing the tell-tale signs of something more than *ganja*.

'Hey Tommy,' said Daniella.

She had always muddled him, but he knew his mum had enjoyed spending time with this new best friend, and he used to love seeing his mum happy. He was scared of Daniella but also hugely attracted to her at the same time, and was totally disgusted with himself for the feeling – however pleasant it was to visualise and re-enact this at night times.

'Fancy a catch up?' She said.

She pointed to her café and he came willingly, never an option to run off or to make excuses.

He may have had all the fancy designer gear, but not the bottle to match, and he needed something familiar.

Something or someone to guide him away from his falling apart. Tommy watched her grab two drinks and loads of cakes and made sure he got the right angle of her backside for that night's entertainment. Daniella watched him in the mirror and shouted to him to stop looking at her ass, and he reddened up, as only a teenager caught in the act can.

'Tommy', said the gorgeous Daniella when she got back to their table with hot chocolates, swirly vegan cream and carrot cakes, decorated with those little green-topped orange iced things that make you feel you ought to be spending your time better.

Like stuffing a mushroom or something.

'Have you noticed anyone hanging round the school pushing anything? I am so concerned that these kids are being abused.'

She didn't say which kid. He wasn't going to answer, he didn't need to. His broad shoulders rounded and his eyes to the table, the constant wiping of the face, the absolute speed with which he ate of all the cakes – definite sign of drug hunger.

So instead, she tried another tactic. She placed her soft ringless-hands, palms down, so close to his he could feel her lovely warmth from them, and she said 'Do you miss your mum?'

And once the tears rolled down his worn-out dear little face, her palms turned up to accept his, and the terrible stories unburdened.

Tommy, like many others before him, fell under her trance, and like the many before, he shared his whole, horrid, heart-breaking story.

THE THERAPIST AND SUSIE

The last time Susie had gone to see her therapist was the day before the accident. Susie had asked Harriet how many narcissists it took to change a lightbulb.

'Just the one, Harry', Susie howled. 'I hold it in place while the rest of the world revolves around me!!' Again, she had talked about death, in her usual unstructured look-at-me manner. Was there anything in what she was talking about of any importance or relevance, and, if so, had Dr Harry missed it? Harriet's day had been much the same as all of her others in the last few years since Manlafi had made it very clear that he couldn't bear to live with her anymore. But was it okay if his mum could stay? The drinking late into the night started earlier every day. Her waking at two or three or four o'clock in the morning, sometimes going back to sleep with the ghosts of all the 'confessions' (as she preferred to think of them) and her own sense of guilt over her inaction, whirring in her head, tormenting her, reminding her of her own failings and ridiculing her many inadequacies.

She knew she ought to have sought out help for herself, if not from the group of supporting therapists, she knew of their existence and earlier on in her new career had played the game of looking like she needed their end of day support, then she should have gone to a different therapist altogether, and outside of this catchment.

She recalled a time when Holly had told her that her friend Susie was looking for guidance, she obviously couldn't tell Holly that she'd known Susie for years, well before Holly had met her. Hell, Susie had even been a plus one at her bogus 'arranged' marriage. Whilst she thanked her for the introduction, Harriet wondered then and now, that if their friendship was as close as Susie had always insisted, then why hadn't she told Holly she was having therapy.

For a lady who was known to tell everyone every single detail, why should this be a secret?

Susie shared most things with most people, except her very best friend it appeared. Depending on her target audience she would either water the story down or dress it up to show how she, Susie, was such a survivor. She may even have tamed the Taliban once, a story borrowed from Daniella.

Susie didn't pay for any of the counselling sessions. They were paid for by her 'benefactor', someone she had really wanted to marry, and he'd been paying since the hasty, short marriage to the second, unfortunate, husband.

It wasn't blackmail, it was just an arrangement, as he had enjoyed the excitement of her, but she wasn't marriage material. He knew she was a tart, but he couldn't stop seeing her.

Dr Harry must have signed some clause back then, agreeing to something on a professional level that meant the sessions were confidential.

The notes were to have been locked away and absolutely no recordings of the sessions, guaranteed.

Well, actually that was supposed to have been the deal, but Harriet had her own instincts and kept these notes in more detail than was originally specified.

They may, of course, prove to play a part in her future dealings with the authorities. They may exonerate her. Or they may hang her.

She often wondered if Susie really thought she needed these sessions or was this to help her build a cover story, to hide the pain of love; perhaps she used this time to build up all of the smoke screens, to test if her lying skills were acceptable and she could convince her therapist.

None of those could be answered by Dr Harry. In all the years of her practice, seeing the murderers waiting for their trials, covering up many times for the paedophile she had married, and counselling the husband-beaters, (more common that suspected) not one of them had ever matched up to the lying and cheating skills of Mrs Susan Bennet.

ROCK ON, TOMMY

After Tommy had told Daniella everything, the horrific details cutting into her own heart, everything from his early sex abuse from her current boyfriend, to the regular visits to their house from Holly's husband and what had happened on the day of his mother's accident; she now knew she had the big secret that Susie had used as the *Damocles* in the first reading of her Will.

This could really ruin Holly's relationship with Susie's fragile memory, but on the other hand, it would certainly be enough for the financial part of the divorce settlement. And she wondered how much of this would have to be shared with Holly. Would the end result be enough?

Now that Daniella was armed with this information, and ready to complete the task she was given so many months ago, she decided to waste no time. She decided there and then to pay Iain Hastings an immediate visit. At his alternative workplace of course, as she knew he was spending more time there than at the Bank. She had always kept her ear close to the ground.

Hindsight would have been to have told someone else she was going, but she chose to tell Manny. After all, they were still in a kind of relationship, although this was now in the misery stages of having invested time, sweat and mad happy-ever-after dreams, the initial attraction had been replaced with the habit of meeting and those hook-ups were getting further apart. And if she was really honest with herself, he was terribly selfish in bed. And now she was aware about his abuse of Tommy.

Manny, never fearful for himself, as his earlier mantra from his mother had wrapped an early warm *Teflon* coat around him, was indeed wary of why she would be going up to the van repainting depot, and not *Itch's* proper office in town. He knew everything that Iain had on him, he had told him often enough. There were plenty of copies made and syphoned away in various bank safe-rooms, lofts, and office desk drawers to protect both of them from each other, but he was sure Daniella would have confronted him directly if this was indeed the real reason for her visit. But, forearmed is forewarned, and Manny called Iain.

Iain Hastings, having already offered Daniella a version of truth was already waiting with blended coffee and twisted good humour. He didn't have an office at the van paint-spraying depot, indeed he thought there was nothing to tie him into the drug running organisation at all, his role was that of the controlling person, not the ultimate beneficial owner – his long experience in banking proved very useful in hiding the money trail. Accumulation and domination in this instance, would never point to him. Well, that was before he started making his coffee dirty with coke.

'My dear Danny-boy' he sang at her as she got out of the low-slung car, her long legs provocative, black, stocking tops showing, such a calculated and obvious tease, throwing him back to the misogynistic borstal-juvenile from Glasgow. He had never been able to truly lose that boy, still hating his mother for his many issues. Hence the childish attempts at an insult. And the easy use of his fists.

Another potential borstal-boy, Tommy, waited in the car, and later Daniella, if she had any reason to, would say he had travelled back with her that day. Never once out of her sight.

'So, when you said, "your son" you meant Tommy?' Hastings laughed and handed her some freshly prepared dirty coffee.

'Tommy the window licker? Ha, he knew about me from years ago. Who do you think went round and shagged his mother as often as I wanted to – even when she first met the footman? He saw me, wanted to make friends, wanted my lifestyle – hell, he may even have told Susie about our little business plans. But she knew better than to say I was their father, I would have cut the money off for all of them – even that skinny girl tried flirting with me when that tart of her mother had her back turned, the fucking mess. Great tits though', he added, almost as an afterthought.

Daniella didn't know who she hated the most right at that moment. Susie for this life-long deception, Iain for lusting after Abigail, his own daughter for God's sake, or the drug empire he must have known would damage thousands of children. Maybe she hated him more for the literal covering up of the van driven by Tommy that had knocked his mother into the promised land. She knew she was going to have to protect Holly from most of this. At any cost.

Tommy had so far managed to stay out of sight in her fancy car. And as with all cyber-savvy teenagers he managed to capture the whole encounter without it being noticed.

He'd had a lot of practice, that way he had kept the dirt on his own runners; and even though he wouldn't know what surreptitious meant, he was certainly a master at it when filming.

He recorded Manny arriving and running over to the pair of them, waving his hands around in a manner designed to bring a plane in to land or to calm a situation. It looked as though Manny was pleading with Daniella and his biological father to come to some sort of arrangement.

Daniella, still the calm one, told Hastings that he must sign the final papers and release the settlement money, plus interest, that same day, and that Manny could draw up all of the paperwork now. That part, of course, would later be edited out of the anonymous file they sent to DCI Lissy Patel.

Hasting's reddened face was building up to an insane black rage – and even Daniella took a step back. He clenched his fists and virtually kicked Manny towards the depot, Tommy guessed for more drugs. He knew a long-time addict and could see the saliva from this distance, so he ensured he zoned in around Hasting's mouth.

'Your boyfriend shagged my daughter as well – do you know that?' He spat at the ex-soldier. 'And your very good friend Susie knew all about it and she didn't tell you.' This technically wasn't possible, as Daniella had met Manny after Susie had died, and they certainly couldn't be classed as good friends. But she decided now was not the time to stop him in his tracks. Never interrupt your enemy when he is off his face, as somebody else once said. Daniella really hoped Tommy was getting all of this.

'He got her pregnant at thirteen' he was raging. 'I paid for that fucking abortion as well, just like every time Susie tried to get pregnant with yet another one of my kids. Trying to get me to marry her.'

Iain's face looked ready to blow up. He was pacing madly, hands shaking and trying to drink his coffee while waiting for Manny to get something, anything. He kept an eye on Daniella in case she was going to attack him. She wasn't. Being able to kill someone doesn't mean you always have to.

'She made me pay out so much money, you know. She blackmailed me for not wanting to marry her, and then threw me aside when the idiotic foot geek tied the knot with her.' He was worked up and sweating and if it was anyone else Daniella would have called an ambulance. But she waited longer. She wanted to see him suffer so much and was almost relieved to see Manny with a plastic bag and a pipe. Give the bastard some more. Please Tommy, get this in focus too.

Later, the edited clip would show Manny Sarr helping Iain Hastings to prepare for his death, against a back - drop from the slowly moving vans, emptying the depot of all the evidence. These would later be recovered but not seen as relevant in that particular police investigation.

Daniella turned to Manny for confirmation that he had got Abigail pregnant at the age of thirteen and made him repeat this until it was word perfect. Tommy captured that too.

212

She turned away from them as her one-time lover was helping his friend into the passenger seat of the nearest Transit van with the intention of drawing up the divorce settlement and transferring the monies. She didn't know it then, and wouldn't have shed any tears if she had, but she was never to see either one of them again.

Afterwards, and far enough away from the scene, Tommy and Daniella worked on the video together until all traces of them or mention of Holly was edited out, and a main copy was to be kept, Tommy's idea, somewhere safe, for protection you know.

Insurances and all of that, said the sad ginger kid from the nice 'hood. They sent the edited version to DCI Lissy Patel via an anonymous IP address from an internet café in an area of Birmingham where she knew, from her military contacts, that there wasn't any street cameras, as this area was under surveillance for terrorists only, not ordinary people like them. If only they knew.

What neither of them realised, was that due to the funding cuts of all the emergency services, resulting in the lack of decent internet provision, along with the necessary expansion of the IT department, (who could have captured every non-recognised IP address, preempting many acts of terrorism), coupled with an insufficient vault capacity, meant that the email they had sent to the DCI that fateful day had gone straight into a junk folder.

And whilst this may eventually be read and acted upon, it would only be as and when the Government department gave the police commissioner more money, and so that particular email was never received by DCI Patel.

Daniella would later send Lissy her own copy, the full and unedited version, after Tommy died.

Later on that dreadful day, Tommy and Daniella went back to her Boho coffee shop where she reset the closed-circuit camera time back two hours, and they spent a nice afternoon smiling and laughing, drinking hot chocolate and eating lots of dry vegan pastries. However hard all of that was.

BREAKING BAD, NEWS

I am so not used to people knocking on the door,
for one thing, how did they get through the gated-
community gate, and for another, my all-singing all-
recording all smart-Alec doorbell was working
perfectly adequately, I'd even had it ping on my
phone but I had been in the far end of the grounds,
cultivating the new apple tree saplings I had stolen
from Susie's orchard before DEFRA reshaped their
garden, and as a result I must have taken longer
than any normal person would have to answer it.
First sign of guilt.
Standing there were two unidentified people, looking
rather dodgy. The older guy, with his designer ripped
jeans showcasing his rather fit legs, had a woollen
beanie hat stuffed under his arm and wore his
emotions clearly, as he rolled-up his shirt sleeves
and nodded to the younger lady who asked me if I
was Mrs Hastings. Now I know I don't look like I
ought to be living in this fancy house, give me a VW
camper van, dungarees and surf-bleached hair (un-
combed, but in great condition) any day, but his tone
was disrespectful, and I retaliated as only a passive-
aggressive social climbing misfit can. I got huffy.
Second sign of guilt.
The gorgeous Indian girl smiled and introduced
themselves as police officers then asked if they
could come in.
I demanded some identification, glanced at it – it
could have been a membership to the last video
shop still open, as it looked that tatty, and then stood
holding the door open while looking out nervously, as
all the people do in the television shows.

Something that until then I thought was ridiculous. How the mind wanders.

'Can you tell me the last time you spoke with your husband' asked the fed-up but fit inspector, who acted as though he didn't want to defer to any female. I asked what this was all about, and he repeated the question.

'Do you mean directly or through the solicitors?' I said, silly response, another sign of guilt. I half expected to be left alone in my garden room while they watched me through the bi-fold windows, so transparent was my immediate guilty reaction.

'Mrs Hastings' said the pissed-off policeman, 'we need to establish your whereabouts earlier today, your husband has been reported missing, and we have reasons to believe he has been murdered.'

I won't say I fell to the floor at this revelation, but I certainly sat down heavily on the nearest chair, where I had left the newly sharpened gardening secateurs moments earlier.

I stood up pretty quickly to remove them from my arse and then slumped back again, breathless, and now in real shock.

'I don't have any direct contact with Iain, he doesn't see the kids as I won't let him. We parted after he tried to strangle me, perhaps you already know this from my report?' By the look they exchanged it was obvious that this was old news, I just had to confirm it for them.

'Check my phone records, check my car computer thing that traces all of my journeys – I haven't spoken to him in months – I don't want to. I have no need to.' I looked at them both. 'Do we want tea or something?'

The female officer nodded to the older guy who didn't disguise his absolute resentment of being sent to do women's work in this woman's kitchen.

She turned back to me and took the gardening tool out of my hand.

'I'm sorry we had to break this to you, Mrs Hastings', she said kindly. 'You know we have to ask these questions. Do you have any idea of who would want your husband dead?'

Give me an A4 pad dear and brace yourself. It would appear that the main suspect is me, the spouse is always the first, opportunity and motive, well, I've got one out of two.

The second person interviewed was his solicitor Manlafi Sarr, as his was the last call to Iain, Daniella told me. This was established after two weeks of waiting for the mobile phone company to release the information, problems with their internet provider or something. Manny didn't mention his girlfriend then (I found out later) so she wasn't questioned as a result of that, but was interviewed at a later stage about something else. I can't recall what that was. Manny was smart enough to know when not to incriminate himself. And as he was already on their radar for his perversions, (I found that out later too!) he charmingly explained that on this occasion he had called Iain with regards to an update on our divorce. The poor boys in blue really do not stand a chance these days.

Tommy was interviewed, along with a responsible adult. Daniella.

Someone said they saw Tommy with Iain on more than one occasion at the paint shop, and on that same day with some 'fit bird'.

This was an anonymous call as it had become well reported by the badly researched late-night news-paper bulletins, that the garage was a cover for the local county-lines trade.

Since Iain had gone missing so too had most of the vehicles (to other repair shops, no doubt to carry on the businesses) and certainly any evidence of drugs or connection to him had gone with them, which was interesting as the authorities were well aware of the activities and had been watching the warehouse for some time – waiting to catch Mr Big. He would have liked that.

Daniella vouched that Tommy had been with her that afternoon, that they had close-camera footage of them having tea at her coffee shop, which was viewed and accepted without question. She was also on the radar, but for the right reasons. No-one could question her integrity, just her taste in Cowboy boots and men.

Iain had ended up in a burnt-out van, the one that had hit Susie all those months ago (we know this now from the footage from the motorway spy cameras the day of her death, and the forensics matching the chips of red Caddy paint) and the Transit had been dumped outside a school in inner-city Birmingham where there had been objections the previous few terms about teaching same-sex acceptance and diversity lessons.

And coincidentally where Manny had started his education when they first moved to the Midlands.

Not that any of that was taken into account, more that the body had been in the passenger seat, leading to speculation that he hadn't driven there and torched himself. Believe me, if he had thought it would have made him money he would have done. As his body was so badly burned, he was identified only by his teeth implants, from one of his many trips to Turkey for the nips and tucks, so there was no way of knowing if he had been bashed on the head or murdered before the van was set alight.

And for that, I really did try to feel something.

A POLICEWOMAN'S WORK IS NEVER DONE

As seen on television, especially on the old programmes based in the gritty South, set in a dark interrogation room, the outside shots panning mainly around a pebbly beach, and those rerun every six hours or so on subscription-free TV, most crime investigations have a glass, if not an interactive, white board, where the suspects' photographs are laid out in a specific manner – who was closest to the victim, who had reason to benefit from this death, emotionally, spiritually or financially.
At this inner-city and much-neglected police station, open usually only on the weekends as that is all the commissioner can afford, his personal chauffeur will attest to that, extra funding had been allocated to allow for the swift conclusion of this particular murder. Unfortunately, access to any broadband wasn't available and the signal to the officer's mobile work-phones was intermittent. But they did have an ancient white board and three wipe-clean marker pens. The extra funding paid for the *Jeyes* cloths.
Murder isn't uncommon in any city, and, as most of the population who take their facts from the main-stream media and the more accurate red-tops will know, it's usually the person closest to the victim that is responsible. Oddly, no-one claimed to be close to Iain Hastings.
The lead duo, the only two officers available to investigate this apparently premeditated crime, as against a spur of the moment bash and torch, were the same two who had visited Holly to break the news in such an unorthodox manner.

Not that anyone would have noticed, as it was all for cause and effect. The end result being that no-one would have willingly sat on a sharp garden tool if they had been guilty, but then they hadn't got to know Holly at that stage, very easy to judge on looks.

On the antiquated and now off-cream board, the Detective Chief Inspector had moved the photos of Holly's two children to the bottom right of Susie's youngest son. A mate from the drug squad had known of Tommy's street activities, they'd had him on their radar while waiting to prove his connection to Hastings' operation, and the colleague kindly alerted Lissy to this.

Abigail so far hadn't had the glory of a place on the board, more than likely due to the many cat filters she added to her Facebook selfies, and 'could they just get an ordinary one please Mrs Hastings?' Until then they would have to make do with a pencil sketch which was fairly accurate, but then only these two well-seasoned officers needed to know who it was. She was on there only because Tommy was her brother. The police officers had seen the reports of Susie's abuse.

Lissy Patel wasn't one of those tired or unlucky in love coppers that every police drama likes to portray. She had a great track record, a spirituality inherited from her calm Indian father, a lust for living, a fondness of *Old Peculier* beer, and a happy, long and solid relationship with VJ, who had herself just been made redundant from an administration role at some rural science place, after getting excited about a *Greasy Pippin*.

After realising how much we are all disposable *Straw Men*, VJ was happily retraining as an art teacher. Lissy meditated on a regular basis, twice daily for twelve minutes, '*I am not this body, I am not even this mind.*' She prepared slow food with humble mindfulness and left her drinking water to stand overnight. Long enough to remember its purpose. Pity we can't do that with people, she said often. She was also a pretty useful painter herself, and she really relied on her ever trusty and over-used gut instincts which was inherent from her ancestors, those older Patels, and their 'positions in leadership'. Her dad had told her to be very proud of her name. And she certainly was.

Her sidekick, on the other hand, hated his surname. He was always over-and-beyond exasperated by virtually anything, to be honest, but was still terrifically gorgeous. Inspector Oliver Tank endured the non-rhyming slang 'I'll have a what?' from the other officers who attempted to try harder at every chance, their West Country accents getting the biggest laughs. But he too was relentless, and his arrest numbers were in the top of the West Midlands Constabulary's ratings for accuracy.

He was Lissy's yang to her yin. The black bit that gradually got whiter as the cases came closer to an arrest, and hopefully leading to a successful prosecution. That part was out of their hands, and it was that part that frustrated Oliver the most.

What was also exasperating was the lack of joined-up operations of all the task forces, drugs, vice, everyday murders and terrorism.

When Lissy and Oliver got the call for this case, they had yet to discover was that Iain Hastings was on a very long list of suspicious activities reports, some almost pre-dating the years of their births. As the two assiduous complementary police officers opened this particular can of worms, the photos of each suspects all merged as one on the old white board. Oliver went to move Tommy's photo underneath a younger one of Iain's. They looked very similar, he said out loud.

'Talk to me' said Lissy. 'Tell me why any of them would have waited so long to get rid of him.'

Oliver did that thing with his hair that only men who were not aware of their own attractiveness could do, hands straight through then it falls right back into place. He stood up, unconsciously mimicking the unfurling and glorious Laurence Fox, as he stretched, clicked his back into position with both hands, and moved to the white board. He pointed to an old photo of Holly.

'Wife', he said. 'Has waited a very long time for a divorce settlement, has inherited her best friend's children and needs the money?'

Oliver waited for a reaction from Lissy, who was positioned with her back straight against a wall, knees bent and in the zone. 'Nope' she said.

'She has her own income from investments at her time in the Bank.' She pointed to a huge printout on her desk.

'I knew of Tommy's mum you know' said the Inspector. Lissy waited.

'In fact, it was when I was seconded to forensics and I first met Jonathan Bennet. He was doing a stint there. A lot of us knew Susie Smith ma'am', he sniggered. 'Ring and ride'. Lissy waited some more. 'I took a call from her and passed her number on to him.' Poor Jonathan, said the expression. Oliver moved on.

'Daniella Ingle certainly has the strength to do this single handed.' Oliver looked over to his boss who now had her legs up against the wall. 'Motive?' she asked. He shrugged.

'Manlafi or Manny Sarr. We know of his interests Lissy.'

Finally, some efficient IT analyst had run the names against the local version of the central PNC database. 'He advised Hastings and may have had some dirt?'

'Hastings was a major prick Olly, he would have had much more on Sarr, some insurances of some kind too, I'd guess. Mind you it would be great to rid the streets of that child-molester.' She swung her legs over her head and stayed like that for a while longer. Blood rush or something. Knees next to her ears.

'It could be more than one of them. Are we in another *Murder on the Orient Express*?'

Lissy had attempted a full circle roll but ended up on her left arm, wincing as she brushed the dust of a thousand investigations from her sleeve and went to the door.

Here she waited before exiting, counted and exhaled to ten in Punjabi, as it takes longer, and came back in, heading straight to the murder board.

She moved Hastings to the top, he would have appreciated this, with Holly, Daniella and Manny in row two.

Beneath those she redrew a more accurate version of Abigail, her brother Tommy had a recent photo from file anyway and this was moved back alongside Abby.

'Who the hell killed you Hastings, you absolute arse', she asked the board.

The answer would come. Until then, she waited for her grumpy sidekick (as she didn't believe in hierarchy) to lock and secure the front door.

She then attached the padlock to the main entrance doors, set an alarm that wouldn't get answered, and treated Oliver to a good long pint at the local pub. Which for some reason had emptied pretty damn sharpish upon their arrival.

SUSIE'S SPAWN

Tommy and Abigail had fought for their mother's attention in the way only neglected children can do. Most of the time though, it wasn't one-child-up-man-ship.

There had been the usual spats where Susie had usually blamed Abigail: 'Well you are the biggest Abigail' she would say, with venom attached to the 'biggest' part of the retort. No, for siblings that had been brought up without love, these two relied on each other in a mysterious way that only a good therapist could attempt to unravel.

The time that Tommy took their mother's car for a spin and Susie held his hand on the engine, it was Abigail who bathed and dressed the putrid burns, making sure when they eventually went to the doctor, as the wound wouldn't stop weeping, that no mention was made of their mother's involvement.

The time after Abby's first abortion and she cried all night, it was kind, confused Tommy who had slept on her floor, bringing her towels when her bed was covered in blood, throwing the sheets into the washing machine before their mother woke up.

Such misplaced kindness from two children who had certainly deserved so much better.

They wouldn't know their mother's actions had been added onto the existing domestic abuser details that Social Services held on Susie. That information would eventually be received by Lissy Patel and Oliver Tank which may have moved the two children temporarily back into pole position, but they didn't stay there for too long, as the officers couldn't guess at any motive, nor opportunity.

Tommy may have been slow, according to the many teachers who wanted to hit the Ofsted targets and who ignored the bright fishes that could swim really well in a smaller pond, but as they couldn't shimmy up the education tree they had to be moulded into something that would ultimately make them feel like failures; but Tommy had been blessed with a great skill. Intermittent listening. Although not always understanding.

He heard the conversations between his mum and Holly. He had always liked Holly, even back then, though he didn't understand initially why her husband only came round when Holly wasn't there.

He listened in on Susie's conversations with Jonathan. Nothing of interest there. Funny that his mother had said the same thing about him too.

He remembered snippets of conversations when Iain Hastings dropped in.

And he dropped in a lot. Sometimes his mum's bedroom door would close, which was quite unusual, and he didn't want to hear what he though was the sound of violence, too much yelling then grunting, so he would get the keys to Iain's latest car, always the top of the range, and would sit in it, sometimes going through the glove compartment.

He would see where Iain had been parking by the discarded tickets or fines in the driver's door pocket.

He listened to the CDs, sometimes music, sometimes just voices, and once he thought he could hear some sex and violence on them.

Hastings wouldn't be listening to *drill* music, would he?

One time Tommy thought he had recognised Abby's voice, screaming out, shouting for help, but he couldn't play it again as he saw the front door opening and knew he had to get out of the car fast. One of his favourite listening pastimes was when Daniella came round. Daniella had been something in the secret service, or so his mum said, this was usually following his bad behaviour and how she would get Daniella to torture him. Not always the worst thought, spending time with her.

Later he would be spending time with Daniella, their dirty secret that one of them would eventually have to give up, but until that point, he had liked Daniella a lot.

By the time of the second reading of Susie's mad Will request, Tommy and his sister had been living with Holly and her two children. It turned out that their dad wasn't their dad, in the biological sense, and that was maybe one of the reasons he hadn't come to get them.

Another reason may have been that their mother's second husband's wife saw the freak that Tommy was trying to control, and didn't want to push that button.

Either way, they got a bedroom and ensuite each at their new home and they could choose their own soft furnishings and furniture, it didn't matter if nothing matched. Holly was odd like that. Loose parenting her own kids had said. *Laissez faire* she called it. She always could depend on her comforting id.

Jonathan had come round a few times, never inside, just to collect Holly to take her out for dinner, a walk, a tree-hugging session, Tommy wasn't too sure now about Holly's mental health.

After all, her husband was dead, the police were crawling all over them and Jonathan was married to his mum. Had been married.

Tommy thought he should ask Abigail about Manny Sarr. He hadn't rationalised about how he should know anything, but he needed a release for his own unidentifiable feelings.

'How did you find out?' Abby asked him, her beautiful eyes blazing with tears.

'Just something I overheard', mumbled Tommy, now realising that the blood on her sheets tied into the sounds of the abuse from the compact disc in the glove compartment of Iain's car, which added up to something that had been rumbling around in his confused slow state of mind for months.

On top of everything, his little foray into the world of building his own empire had been halted, his supply was intermittent, his drug withdrawal affecting his rational mind, and his emotions were running rife.

No amount of therapy could alter the fact that he had killed his mother, and his father's closest ally had raped his sister, more than once.

Something had to give.

POLICE PARADOXES

DCI Lissy Patel was trying to allow the blood to come quicker to her brain by balancing on her head on a rough seat cushion against the incident room's furthest wall, as Oliver brought in some take-out coffees from Daniella's Boho shop. He hadn't realised this was a vegan place and so had opted for coconut milk in the hope that he could actually drink it. Thank goodness the previous investigation had left a load of sugar in the cupboards.

He chipped away at the solid grey lumps in the still dank bag while watching his boss go red in the face.

'Why isn't the therapist on our list Olly?' Lissy asked, when gracefully, for once, she rolled out of this variation on a theme of some yoga stance.

'She was married, may still be, to the child molester, she was therapist to Susie Bennet and Holly Hastings, and she guarded that old Gambian thief. Why would she keep Kaddy Sarr? There's got to be a link, surely?'

Oliver said it probably made good sense to talk to her, shed some light where allowable, therapist rules of what's said in therapy stays in therapy, and this caused Lissy to give him a long hard look and ask if he'd ever had any.

'Of course I have,' he said, 'to find out why I'm so loveably bad-tempered.' He then smiled that smile which always worked, even on Lissy, which had shocked her the first time, although she made sure she had discussed this with VJ. Victoria had just laughed.

He suggested that they both went over to the ex-GP's house and spring a nice surprise on her.

'One lump or two boss?'

Taking their disgustingly sweet coffees with them, and Oliver driving whilst illegally holding his sticky cup, Lissy told him about the time they first had Manlafi Sarr on the radar and how, as a young officer she had been given the task of talking to Harriet Palmer about his misconduct.

She had spent most of that time trying to get the GP to like her, chatting about spiritual things, being a therapist, water and all that, but there was something behind the genial front that was rocking the boat. Lissy actually snorted at that.

Oliver said that was 'very interesting' in the style of every text-book therapist and this rightly warranted a punch on his arm from his boss, spilling his tepid coconut concoction into his lap.

Upon arrival at Harriet Palmer's house, they couldn't help but notice this was moving day. Maybe the three removal lorries parked illegally gave it away, they hadn't needed training to spot that.

The inspector parked on the drive, much to the annoyance of the gaffer, who swiftly turned his attention to the restocking of the untaxed lorries into the nearest one, so at least that could be moved, hopefully before they got rumbled.

Oliver automatically ran the number plates through the system.

Dr Harry had always relied on her instincts, whether she acted on them or not, and had been surprised that she hadn't yet had a visit from the fuzz;

after all, her husband was in the frame for the death of Hastings, being the last one to have seen him alive, allegedly.

She went to the open door to find the gorgeous policeman about to ring the antique bell.

'Where do they get these idiots from?' was her first, thought. She waved impatiently at them both to hurry up and come in.

After being shown into what was previously the consultation room, the one that looked out over the many dead plants in random broken plastic pots, and a huge bonfire in the garden, Oliver excused himself, pulling the cold, wet cloth away from his sticky crotch, and made his way to the galvanised metal incinerator carefully kicking this over to ensure nothing further could be burnt.

His eyes were on Harriet in the house during this time, and he thought he saw some reaction when he started rummaging through the scarred debris with an unburnt metal walking stick of Kaddy's, but would wait to hear what Lissy had discovered.

The Detective Chief Inspector was reminding Harriet of the last time they had met.

'Do you still leave your water to find its purpose', she asked. Harriet said yes, she did, we are made of water, and the taste was satisfying and the drink more rewarding. Answered like a child trying to impress her teacher.

Lissy then asked her what she was burning. It wasn't a police trick to change the subject so quickly, she used it with her staff too, but it always worked.

The most typical responses were usually wrapped within so many lies that could soon be twisted and dismissed, these would be then followed with a long run of words that made no sense whatsoever, then, perhaps, a misdirected half-truth resulting in what could have been achieved from the onset.

But that was other people.

'Sage?' Harriet said. Then: 'Actually, papers I no longer need' said this trustworthy therapist.

'Anything in that bin belonging to Manlafi Sarr, Dr Palmer?' asked DCI Patel.

She watched the range of emotions flit over the other woman's face. The swallowing of excess saliva from the karmic-water helping her to form some words.

'Yes', she said.

TOMMY'S TROPHY

It wouldn't have been any great surprise to Manny
when Tommy called at the office. They went back a
long way after all. Manny had most recently supplied
leads to Tommy, as he liked to call it, and always had
an ever-present supply of the drug *du jour*.
And once, they may have had a thing for each other.
Tommy being too young and unloved to understand
the long-term consequences of the older man's
actions. Other than it hurt a lot to sit down
afterwards.
Today however, Tommy wasn't looking for validation,
sex, or for friendship.
He wanted to beat Manny's head in for preferring his
sister to him and getting her pregnant. The underage
stuff was on record and was already sent to the
police, they had thought.
Daniella had urged him not to give Manny any
inclination. In fact, she had told him to steer well
clear of the snake. Tommy wasn't one for taking
guidance.
Tommy wasn't very bright you see, in spite of his
street smarts, and Manny had dealt with and paid off
more angry siblings and their greedy parents than
even he cared to recall.
All the same, smart or not, Tommy had watched
enough late night crime dramas on Netflix and had
made sure he'd worn the skin-coloured latex gloves
that he had earlier stolen from Jonathan's work
office, before he entered Manny's very OCD clean
and private den. Some things ran in the family.

When Iain Hastings had ever cut any type deal, he kept many copies of all the evidence so that he could later use against people, if required.

For every occasion where either himself or someone close to him had screwed up, he gave to Manny, as his unofficial solicitor, a spare copy, just for future insurance sakes.

The threat of exposure was often more than enough, the actual files untouched for many years.

Manny's spare copies were sitting gathering dust in his ex-wife's loft, some others in this office, and most of Iain's at his Law Society's kosher solicitor's practice. Filed away and probably forgotten, and possibly under a pseudonym.

Unbeknownst to Tommy, DCI Patel and Inspector Tank were at this moment sifting through the sooty remains of the USB sticks, CDs and papers, all recovered from Harriet's incinerator, and had instructed a load of SOCOs to go through everything left in her loft. Kaddy Sarr's mementos included.

Dr Palmer was in the process of being escorted to another Police Station while this preliminary investigation was carried out.

'Tommy my boy' said Manny with that fabulous private school twang, mixed with the BBC coveted received-pronunciation accent he overuses.

'How are you holding up?'

He offered some soft drinks from the huge fridge and pointed to the spirit dispensers for Hastings' son to help himself, giving Tommy a glimpse of Iain Hasting's gun that he had appropriated from the burnt-out van on the day that Hastings had died.

'I was wondering if the *Old Bill* have figured out that you were driving the Transit on the day your lovely mamma died?" Wrong-footing him as intended.

'Iain kept a copy, a record of everything', Manny was saying.

'Every meeting, every bribe, every wrong-doing – my goodness he even kept a video recording and a scribed copy of when your mum confronted him about me getting your sexy sister up the duff, that was worth twenty-five grand to her, plus the damn fees to get rid of my devil child!!'

He was actually laughing, inviting Tommy to appreciate the cunningness of the now, thankfully dead, Iain Hastings.

Tommy, with shaking hands but admirably controlled anger, carefully poured himself a huge vodka, not the decent stuff Jonathan had, more like the fake fair-trade Russian stuff produced locally, (it was well known to be mixed with an inferior brand but marketed appropriately to the faceless braggarts who shopped at the exclusive fancy emporiums and thought they knew their stuff).

He emptied a can of very cold lemonade into a long cut-glass tumbler, adding some ice from the top compartment of the fridge.

He saw himself in slow motion as he half turned back to Manny, holding the still mostly full artisan bottle by the neck and smashed it onto the marble counter before thrusting it with full force into the child molester's astonished face.

He watched himself in slower motion ripping the cameras from the corners of the office and the reception area, logging onto the computer and erasing any trace of himself.

Susie's son may have been slow, but he was a half-decent technophile.

Going back into the office, Tommy pushed the blood-splattered blue ergonomic chair around so abruptly that Manny's limp but not-dead-yet body fell to the lush wool-carpeted floor with just a slight thud, and he watched himself grind the bottle further into the pervert's neck with his boot, and then, with each of his *Doc Marten's* he took it in turns to kick his and his sisters abuser's face into a pulp, finally jumping repeatedly onto the length of the body with his full weight, until he was sure that every bone in Sarrs' body had snapped.

Afterwards, placing the gun in the child-abuser's hand, Tommy poured the vodka cocktail onto the shattered, torn penis of the vile paedophile, emptied Manny's drug stash into his pockets, and took his glass home to Holly's.

A trophy, his mum would have said. Pity he forgot about the lemonade can.

MANLAFI SARR NEEDS HIS WIFE

Manny Sarr had sailed through life because his
mother, like most single parents, carried the guilt of a
thousand ancestral failures. And some of her own
making. By defending him and protecting him, she
could diminish her culpability as a provider.

Had she loved him, and had she not known for sure
that he was the work of the Protestant devil himself,
thereby excusing his actions even as a child, she
would have sought out professional help at an early
age. Or even just plain acceptance.

Once she found him dressing up as her, she ought
not to have put this down to his missing his mother –
she was certain that this was because he could
smell her through her clothes. She could have either
supported him in his own sexuality – unheard of that
a child of hers could be queer, or beat the hell out of
him. She chose to use the violence. As was the
innate ancestral way of this *namp*.

Knowing that his mamma would always assuage his
behaviour, and that the beatings were given in love,
he knew this because she never told him so, and
accepting she would protect him without exception,
was one of the reasons he agreed to get Harriet to
marry him. Another protective woman.

The other reason for marrying a GP, in his defence,
was to treat his many diseases he brought home to
her, although he hadn't realised that was such a
bonus when he first met this stomach-turning, dick-
limping, frumpy freak.

It was for the mother-figure reason that he had turned to his estranged wife on the day that Iain Hastings overdosed.

Harriet happily took his call, it always gave her some false hope that they would fall back in love, that he would stop shagging anything and everyone, but this dream was only for a fraction of a second. She already knew of his many perversions and these recorded deeds on the videos that she was desperately trying to hide. She should have done this a lot earlier. Burn his actions and her associated guilt. Soon it was to be the only thing they ever really shared.

'Harry, baby' he had said. 'I need the biggest favour from you. *Itch* is dead and I'm on camera as maybe the last person to have seen him. I need an alibi. Please baby, for me.'

When Harriet didn't immediately respond he asked if they could meet somewhere away from it all, maybe the house? He had to see her; it could all go really wrong for both of them.

As Harriet was already in the process of moving right away from him, the house papers exchanged and a completion day set, she may have thought to herself 'what's the harm?'

Maybe she thought that by laying this warped ghost to rest she could start mixing the artisan jams and reading all of the books she promised herself she would have taken to her own *Desert Island*. But, as Harriet Palmer wasn't anybody's fool, she wasn't going to allow him to come to the house – what else could he hide? So instead she said she would meet him in his office. She knew the cameras worked there.

Within an hour she had parked outside his building, under a not-so-covert CCTV camera, which was pointed right at the main entrance to Manlafi's offices, carrying a paper bag full of his 'things', as an excuse, she could have said if challenged, after all, the protective order he had issued against her in the early days of their separation was yet to expire.
As Manny went to hug her, she held the bag out at arm's length.
'These are yours' she said. 'Lots of evidence in there, I've watched some of them and you are a disgusting human being. I hate you.'
Manny pretended to appear chastised as he took the bag from her and put it on the marble counter. He offered her a drink, knowing she couldn't refuse. Always the narcissist. Always the drunk.
'Babe, you knew all of this all along, that's why you married me! You could have saved me! What about when you lied to that gay Indian girl for me – you are just as involved baby face. Anyway, who needs to bring all that up now, I really did try to love you the most,' he said as he brought the chilled New Zealand wine in a fancy goblet over to her.
'Which is why I need your help now.'
Was it really enough, she wondered, ever fascinated to watch him in action.
'What have you done now, Manlafi?' she asked.
'He had too much crack-cocaine Harriet, baby.'
She loved when he fell into the Banjul accent that neither he nor his mother had. He knew it seduced her, she knew he knew, but God did she need some validation for her whole life.

'*Itch* was already loaded by the time the tranny and the kid got there. I brought him some more, because he yelled for some more, baby I didn't want to, you do understand I hate the stuff don't you, and then he just keeled over. Started frothing at the mouth, he was twitching when his eyes went back into his head, oh babe it was really scary for me but I helped him into the van and dumped him outside my old school. I torched the van Harry; I didn't know what to do – I was driving it. It was hot anyway. I need an alibi.'

Looking at the man who had taken away any last sense of decency from her, she will never know why she said: 'Tell me exactly Manlafi, the time frames, the journey you took there. Why that school? How did you get back? Everything.'

And, as every woman who has ever been destroyed by love will surely understand, she planned his alibi, his journey home away from public transport, and she sorted his story to the police, should it be needed.

His old elementary school, where he had suffered the daily bullying from the non-white kids, for his skin colour, for having a single parent, but mostly for enjoying the diversity lessons. For once in his life he had felt included. It sounded pretty accurate on paper. She hoped he wouldn't ham it up.

Harriet then helped to destroy as much of the evidence that Iain had saved, copies from the filing cabinets in the storage rooms she loaded into her car to burn later, and deleted everything on the computer hard drive. Removing the trashed documents too.

241

She wasn't as savvy as today's teenagers but thought she had done enough.

What she had unknowingly done by removing the files and the cache that the deleted files fell into, was to activate the live feed software hidden deep behind all of the back doors to the security firewall, put there one day upon Hastings' instructions and without Manny's knowledge. This linked to a security system and would carry on playing, being backed up by some third-party technology, even if the computer was not switched on.

And as luck would have it, for anyone who needed this particular blessing, the latest *Nintendo* long-awaited fantasy game had been released the day of Tommy's visit, and due to popular demand, judging by of the amount of people downloading it, everyone's broadband was really slow; so fortunately for Tommy, when he went to Manny's private den later, his entrance was the last thing backed up and stored away on a *Cloud* somewhere in a supercomputer's automation.

Everything after Harriet's visit was being broadcast out live, but not recorded. And the total real-time destruction of Manlafi Sarr went unobserved.

Harriet didn't care that she was over the legal alcohol limit. She felt like she had finally done something worthwhile. She drove home to prepare for the next bonfire.

Bonfire of the vanities she laughed out loud in the car. No-one more deserving than Kaddy Sarr's sick and unwanted son.

POLICE STRIKE

Inspector Oliver Tank was at the point beyond toleration. He always was, to be fair, They had pulled Dr Palmer in for some serious questioning but how come neither of them had discovered the details of the restraining order?

They'd already told the guardian of the pursestrings that they had needed more manpower to go through the backgrounds of the few suspects before the interviews, or at the very least, give them decent internet access and they would do it themselves. Money saved in one way adds to extra time costs later. Basic business sense, VJ had said to Lissy.

'We got a *Jeyes* cloth though', smirked Oliver.

Harriet Palmer was both happily confused and perplexed. The police officers wondered how on earth the doctor's husband had got a restraining order out on her rather than her on him, as by now they all knew of Manny Sarr's extra-curricular activities – just not the minutia, which, thankfully, was left for another department to scrutinise.

'I really don't know how I can help you any further, officers', she said, getting more comfortable with her position, both with the chair and her well-prepared story.

She shuffled about pulling her bonfire smoked and stained, dark blue and extra-large fisherman's jumper down over the fat pants, in an attempt to hide the quite disturbing and cellulite-riddled muffin top.

'He moved out and I was clearing all of his clutter from the loft. Cathartic Lissy, you understand?'

Lissy said she did.

243

'He had some work stuff which I am sure was out of the retention date, his old clothes and papers were of no use to me. He'd had the chance to get them for some years, I just assumed that they were of no use to him and I wasn't taking them with me, so I dropped them over to his offices.' Realising she was offering more than was necessary, rather than waiting for a direct line of question, she faded away slightly for a split second.

DCI Patel poured her some more water. Fresh from the hot-water tap in the Ladies' loo, as the cold tap had been snapped off. Great recovered memories from the old lead pipes straight in the single-use plastic beaker.

'Dr Palmer, Harriet' said Lissy. 'We believe your husband was one of the last to see Iain Hastings alive, anything we can get to support his lack of involvement in the murder can only help him.'

Harriet immediately looked up at the lovely Indian girl.

'What makes you say it was murder?' she asked, and gave the whole game away.

All of the media outlets had been instructed to classify this as a murder. The exhausted PR guy for the police had pushed this detail, so they had no idea it was anything else, and the laziness of criminal journalists these days was measurable by taking the statements verbatim. They'd learned from investigating the Oligarchs and having their lives threatened, that it wasn't worth exposing anything that their editors and owners didn't want publishing. So why would the media think otherwise and push for anything factual?

The body was found on the passenger seat. He hadn't driven there, moved seats and set fire to the van now had he?

Lissy turned the recording equipment off and asked for her Inspector to step outside with her as she slapped her hand to her forehead, initially for dramatic purposes and to hopefully knock some sense back into herself. She cuffed it so hard she left an actual handprint. And through the deserved and resulting pain Lissy asked Oliver if it actually had to have been murder.

Oliver walked her back to the investigation room and pointed to the various photos on the sad, old, white board. One by one. Holly, Manny, Daniella, the children.

'I don't think so' he finally said.

With nothing being recoverable from Iain's body, and without the forensic experts available in those US television dramas to rehydrate and extricate some bodily fluids, they couldn't actually prove this was a homicide. Maybe it was simply an accident. A cover up.

A lucky break is what most police investigations relied on and it was at this point that a young civilian who had recently applied to join the force and was currently manning the phones, caught up with them with a piece of paper in her hand. Also, with the urgent message: 'Suspect Manlafi Sarr was found dead in his office this morning, by the cleaning lady – it's messy apparently. The ambulance is on its way now.'

With the biggest sense of sadness as she reopened the door to where Harriet was still sitting, Lissy stood next to the failed therapist and asked her why she had broken her restraining order by going to see Manlafi.

Harriet managed to look confused long enough for Oliver to momentarily doubt Lissy's usually excellent tactics, and then Lissy, avoiding all eye contact with the doctor, decided to hit her with the brutal news of her husband's death.

Whilst doing so she glanced down at the piece of paper she had kept from the messenger. It read 'Sarr's computer is broadcasting live, send the IT nerd over ASAP'.

Handing Oliver the note, Lissy sat down with Harriet. The shock of hearing the words that Manny was dead, that and the fact of defying her restraining order, may have broken a lesser person.

But Harriet Palmer had been empty on the inside for a long time, probably why she said she'd never needed to recover from her patients' tales of woe, and relied on her warm wine instead, and so when Lissy repeated her question, Harriet Palmer simply said he had called her and asked her for help. Which was the truth.

DANIELLA'S DOG

It was a perfect rainy afternoon for self-indulgence. The stylish cream curtains were thrown wide open and she was sitting alone in her enviable top-floor apartment that faced out onto the canal systems of Birmingham. Daniella had never rid herself of that big black dog of depression. Today he was pacing. She had lit a bergamot candle to honour her mixed emotions and poured another finger or two of a very fine malt, available only from a remote island in Scotland, in the misguided hope of drowning her constant misgivings. Contrary coping mechanisms of course, but her heart was full of the many wrong doings she had witnessed throughout her transitions, and those she had committed in warfare. She hoped anything would help hush that dog up.

Those early adaptations from unloved and unwanted son to emotion-free soldier. Never knowing her biological dad. Would things have been different with that knowledge? She thought she was the one who had abandoned her parents in Yorkshire but when they hadn't made too much of a fuss, she knew it was only another cut to her already damaged heart. On her way to the metamorphosis of becoming the confident and beautiful Daniella, steadfastly shedding each of her journeys like yesterday's perfect cocoon, she had failed many times.

Unfurling those steely butterfly wings to become her idea of who she knew that deep down she really was, and that she had always been.

Travelling on this turbulent coast road round her life she also knew that she could never unburden these secrets on to anyone, therapist or friend.

247

They would have to keep hidden away forever, and therefore she would be visited by that flipping dog for life.

She may as well name him for all the time they spend together. Daniella remembered someone once saying that you should chose to be melancholic as that was something you were. Rather than be depressed, as that is something you have. So she decided to call the dog Melon Collie. Not original. Daniella knew that by sharing anything that really mattered about herself, or her experiences, she would un-write her own script. Her many versions of who she really wanted to become. In the end.

So many works in progress she was once told by the fabulous plastic surgeon, who loved her new tits, she added. Stories that Dan had rewritten many times to convince herself she was really doing great, better than great. Putting that out to *The Universe.*

Maybe she was more like Susie than she had recognised in herself.

And suddenly she felt an overwhelming sadness over her recent lack of judgements, her failed relationships. She loved little Holly in the way only a woman can love another, maternally, passionately, deeply and protectively. She had wanted to love Manny, maybe once she could have done, but the blackness of his soul had permeated through to hers.

Right through her and still feeding the depressive Collie.

When she was rational and without emotion, she knew she could be objective in her thoughts, that she could see herself outside of them.

Now she just wanted to be in the newly washed air and armed with a very strong coffee because she needed to show some love to Susie. Susie had become Daniella's nemesis. And not the fun ride at that theme park either.

At the heart of everything that was now blackened in Daniella's world was the scheming lies and the webs of deceit that Susie had started all those years ago. The cobweb spun, ruthlessly silky and strong, without any regard for those she caught and trapped along the way. And even when she could have tried to make everything good again, she chose to wrap more misery around the pain, including her own. Isolating people from whichever vintage of her authentic self, by trying to get them to love yet another cover version. Wow, that sounds familiar, said Daniella to the dog.

There was no doubt that Tommy had sent his mother to her death. And he was rapidly going downhill as a result of that, and recently finding out about Manny's abuse of his sister. She wished he hadn't heard that. Somehow though, Tommy hadn't minded her own short relationship with Manny. Or that could have been just an act, as he was now totally dependent on Daniella protecting him, and showing him the next moves.

Had Tommy killed his mother or had Susie killed herself by her own carelessness? Better wait for the courts to decide. The implication of his mother's relentless abuse may be taken into account as the reason he was off his face on class A drugs so early on that fateful morning. Something that may lessen his sentence for that particular charge.

Daniella thought about Holly wanting Jonathan to come back and rescue her. She doesn't see the consequences of this. Harbouring two criminals in her life. Tommy will go off the rails eventually, absolutely no doubt about that. Daniella had seen the crime scene photos from Manny's murder, she had kept in touch with her police sources, even pointlessly flirting with the despondent Inspector Oliver Tank to try and lighten the mood.

The destruction of Manny's perfect face and body had seen her excused to run to the gender-neutral lavatory in the police station to throw up. Lissy had held her long hair back for her and rubbed her shoulders, waiting for the retching to stop.

If only Tommy hadn't confessed his reasons for the destruction to Daniella, and therefore reminding them of her own role in setting this all off, plus, of course, the evidential copies of the recordings, then she may not have toyed with the notion of keeping his involvement a secret.

Her non-emotional head said that she would, of course, have to tell Lissy and Oliver everything; she had no choice.

Surely Manny had deserved to die. Now she was empathising with Jonathan's predicament.

Is the end result always justified? In Manny's case he had destroyed many young and old people's lives.

He took Abigail's virginity and raped her on more than one occasion, confirmed with little thanks to his deranged therapist of a wife keeping some of his most sickening USB sticks. For her own protection, Dr Palmer had told Inspector Tank.

Harriet was on her way to getting sectioned, and possibly let off the hook, so confused was her rationalisation. Manny's continuing abuse resulting in at least one of Abby's abortions, to Daniella's knowledge. What kind of mother was Susie to allow so much suffering? Much later when Daniella watched Abby's reaction to the news of his death, she could see the confused relief and gratefulness, with a touch of sadness, written all over her beautiful and gaunt face. As well as betrayal. Daniella wondered then if by sleeping with Hasting's daughter Manny was in fact shafting Iain. Maybe theirs was a love unspoken.

Fucking poetic licence, she said out loud. The black dog didn't need to add anything. They were evil men whose actions would have continued to destroy everything lovely in their paths. A long, lonely legacy. For what? Power? Money?

The records Iain Hastings had meticulously kept were still being analysed by the ex-military staff, employed as their experiences of war had left them devoid of all emotion. Such as Daniella's lack of deep feelings, she had suffered the same, war was good for nothing. She had really tried to love. War was the destruction of people's lives, whatever side of misplaced honour they thought they were fighting on.

Hasting's documentation was being cross-referenced with Manlafi Sarr's own safety records, his insurances; the ones saved from Harriet's pathetic last act of trying to protect her hateful husband by attempting to burn them on the bonfire.

Incriminating herself in the process, without a doubt. Guilty by association.

One by one the dots were joining up in the most horrid of stories. This story would never be made into a blockbuster, no one would want to play the disgusting men and the manipulative women in this whole, sad story.

Holly had to be kept away from all of that. She had suffered enough. During her official interview into the suspected murder of Iain, Daniella had spoken with Lissy and Oliver in great detail about the gas-lighting Holly had experienced throughout her marriage.

The duo knew of Daniella's high regard by the various agencies and her secrecy missions in the military and decided that these references would be enough to, if not exonerate Holly totally as the questions would still have to be asked, then definitely they could exclude her from the centre of the white board.

For Daniella to protect her best friend going forward, she had to get Susie's children away from Holly and her own sweet children.

She had to get Holly over to America and for her to have her own sense of happy ever after. But life wasn't working out like that. She knew that Tommy guessed what Daniella was planning, he listened at doors and broke into computers and was off his head more times than he was rational, no matter how much effort Holly made with him. How long would it be before he flipped on me?

Perhaps it was time to take the black dog out for a good long walk. Maybe see if she could push him into one of the canals and hold his head under the murky depths.

She could go to her gym and see how the staff had been faring in her absence and she would shake off her own doubts, maybe do some yoga stretches and then get some insurances in place. She would talk to Oliver.

As she went to charge her laptop up she thought she heard a knock at the door.

Not expecting anyone, she peeped through the spy hole, hesitating just long enough to turn the internal recording camera on, before unlocking the many security devices, one by one.

HOLLY'S HEART IS BROKEN

Dear Reader, I didn't marry him. Or, at least I should
say, I haven't married him yet, although that's mostly
because he hasn't asked me.
He went to America as the FBI guys loved his stuff
and he set up in business there. It had always been
his plan. He told me on an early date that he wanted
to go international, Australia was mentioned back
then too. Apparently feet are becoming the next big
forensic thing.
He is also teaching at a well-established Ivy League
university where no doubt a gorgeous blonde
Californian girl will fall in love with him – maybe more
than one. He is very easy to fall in love with.
How very of me silly for not knowing this earlier.
I get daily emails and regular face calls, these
sometime last for hours into the night and I get to
visualise that he's here with me. I am hoping to go
over next month, subject to getting the visa and
whether the zealous USA border control allow me to.
Me, a person of interest linked to a number of
suspicious activities. Most exciting thing that's ever
happened in my life!
When the DCI came to tell me about Iain and asked
if I had anyone who could stay, I immediately called
Daniella.
She arrived within the hour looking very angry with
Lissy and her inspector, and burdened with
something else. I never did ask what it was and she
never volunteered anything either.
She said hello to Abigail and nodded to her brother.

Before Jonathan went to America, and since the year was up and Susie's infamous part two of the Will was read, such an anti-climax – it turned out her kids aren't her second husband's, and would I take them to live with me?

Too late, I said, as they'd already moved in. Didn't I say 'Don't leave me your children Susie!!' She'd had the last laugh, as usual.

Her second husband Andrew and I had finally had the chance to catch up. I suspected that he'd initially come to me looking for funding for his wife's IVF treatments, Susie's kids had heard about this and had enjoyed telling me that they may soon have a 'brother by another mother'.

I suspected he was going to guilt me into opening my purse, maybe he thought he knew something I didn't, but by then I wasn't really that bothered either way and perhaps when he realised that, he recognised the futility of his action. When I questioned his sperm count, something you can only do with someone if you really don't give a shit, he said he had always been infertile, a nasty dose of mumps when he was small.

He's still small to be honest. I didn't give him any money and he didn't give me anything I didn't already know.

As I'd already had Abigail and Tommy staying with me for the weeks before the second Will reading, and they'd initially acted as though they were excited to stay here, we all agreed to make this a permanent thing.

Fortunately for me, my kids hadn't objected too much. Well, they did actually, quite a lot, as my son has never liked Tommy. My aim is to keep them well apart thanks to the extra money for all of their extracurricular activities! Abby has been a godsend with the cleaning too. I feel she has morphed into a mother role, so totally opposite to her own, and intends to look after me. I enjoy it to be honest.

We had all moved into a much bigger house, again thanks to Iain leaving me everything.

Well, almost everything. His accountant via the solicitor, or the other way round, had suggested that since Susie's kids were now in my care, or they were my ward or something, it would make good tax sense to ensure all the four children had their own trust fund set up for them.

One thing I have always known is that I could rely on Iain's fabulous and legal tax-avoidance knowledge, so I agreed to this, madness not to really. It must have been very well laundered by the time it got to us. Iain was master of that also. He taught me a lot. Tommy bothers me though. Even now I can see his path to prison. He has a fabulous en-suite room, I gave him carte blanch again to decorate it exactly how he wanted. That was a big mistake unless black is the new black.

He also had strict instructions to not smoke – anything – in there, he doesn't, he does it outside, leaving the nub-ends in my herb pots. I don't think he has ever really recovered from his mum's death.

I hear his tears but always wait to be asked to come in. They never had privacy at home, his sister once told me, Susie insisted on all the bedroom doors being left open, hers included.

I had arranged for some private tuition to try and get Tommy some qualifications, restore some sense of his self-worth I had hoped, and I also introduced him to our brand-new cognitive behaviour therapist, recommended by Dr Harry before she went crackers.

That old fraud has completely disappeared from my life. I hardly think about her now, which apparently isn't the way to deal with it. Neither is visiting her in the open prison where they are keeping her locked up until it's all sorted, and they can transfer her to a secure unit for mentally impaired.

I actually laughed out loud when I heard that my therapist was pleading innocent due to some mental defect. Insane.

I may send her a cake and put a saw in it, or something. Maybe some more of the Valium she had pushed on me over the many years, I could disguise it again in the sticky mixture. I had done that more than once, it was fun to watch her lose control of her words. The sad and silly old fool, she never had a clue about me.

The CBT lady is helping all of us now, with coping mechanisms and bringing emotions to the surface, and Daniella was keeping a close eye on us too, but I hadn't heard from her in a while.

I think she became quite sad when Manny was murdered, I had hoped she had found true love – that was one sexy guy I can tell you!!
I used to always manage to say hi when I went round to do his mum's accounts. Back then, they were all happy to live rent-free with Harriet.
I made a note to go and see Daniella. I miss her.
And I miss Jonathan too. So much that it hurts to breathe some days. I miss his calmness. I miss his lovely smart mind and his thoughtful words, no throw-away comments from him, just reflective, measured responses.
I miss the way he holds me, the way he makes love to me in the middle of the night, so gently, and in the middle of the afternoon, when he fights me off, like a caveman.
And I miss the way he covers me with his old and comforting cardigans whenever I feel the chill of something long gone run right through my cold bones.
A long-gone goose walking over my grave.
Yes, he's back to the old cardigan wearing Jonathan, the one pre-Susie's moulding into her version of Mr Perfect.
But to me, he is my Mr Perfect, and I fear I will lose the only man I've truly loved.

THE POLICE AND MORE DREADFUL NEWS

When DCI Patel had come to Holly's new address, an established old mansion this time, to inform her of Tommy's attempted murder of her friend Daniella, she brought the lovely Oliver too. Mainly because he was worth looking at and secondly, she was there to deliver some more bad news, and while this wasn't her first time of breaking such sadness, she had grown fond of Holly and so she may even cry herself.

'Hey Holly,' said the lovely and calm Lissy. 'Can we come in?' Holly didn't need to look down her estate this time as their new home was in plenty of land of its own, no neighbours to overlook her imaginary misdoings, but still, she did.

The police duo followed Holly down the huge, almost mile-long hall, (it seemed) passing a quiet den on the left that she had made her own, away from the outside cruel world, protecting her with its whacky curtains and mismatched rugs, her nan's cake recipes, her investment books and hundreds of rubbish chick-lit novels, but still, from this wonderful vantage point, she was able to see the comings and goings of the four non-harmonious teenagers.

They passed another smaller bolt hole, this one for anyone who needed the zen within, Lissy could feel the energy as she walked past, and then they all continued down into the enormous designer kitchen. This room was bigger than Lissy and her fiancée's whole terraced-house in a developing part of Birmingham.

That happy couple shared a converted three-storey house with huge ceilings, and the high walls all now covered with VJ's art. She was setting up an online store too, having already sold fair-trade-is-local-trade to the fancy bistros on behalf of the Birmingham born immigrants so that they could fund their airfare home.

On the patio in very large pots, VJ had planted the apple seeds that she had taken from her last job, as a hasty leaving present, smuggling the remaining *Greasy Pippin* core in her coat pocket, and they were multiplying nicely. All was very well in Lissy's world, even some talk of bringing the marriage forward.

Holly filled the fast-boiling eco-friendly kettle straight from a tap, and after noticing her new eco-partner-in-crime's look of horror, she explained it was pre-filtered.

There was a machine fitted to the mains system at source to ensure all the drinking water had its impurities removed. Any gunk is then treated before going back into the septic tank system to further break down the residue; before re-joining the sewerage works and hopefully avoiding any further chemical cleansing before being used as organic matter fertiliser for the farmers no longer getting their EU subsidies.

Such advances when you have nothing else to spend your money on, was written all over the Inspector's dour face. No time for recovered memory, though, thought Lissy. Saving the planet, was thrown back at them from Holly's.

They drank their impurity free tea in another wing of the kitchen, it did indeed taste amazing, said Oliver, and they sat on low, but really comfy, multi patterned expensive settees and partook of a freshly baked carrot cake. With her homemade sticky icing and those mad trademark carrots that she does on the top. Such a lovely setting to deliver such a terrible message.

'Holly' the DCI said, as she reached over to hold her hand. 'I'm so sorry to have to tell you that Tommy is dead.' Holly's little face crumpled as she tightened the hold on Lissy's hand, noticing the pointlessly small diamond in her engagement ring and asked if she should call Daniella.

'Holly, Daniella was attacked by Tommy, she is now in the city hospital. She put up a good fight. Is there anyone else you can get to come over?'

Holly ordered a taxi for her only other companion; her mother, her final ally.

Oliver took over the hand-holding and told her what they knew so far. They believed that Tommy had killed Manny Sarr, they had found evidence pointing to the boy being the last person to see him.

A discarded can of pop, or some computer stuff. Oliver didn't mention the photographs of Tommy's brutal destruction of Manny. He still felt sick at the thought of having to go through them again, to ensure they captured every detail, to hazard a guess at a time line, they knew when Tommy had entered Manny's office and the estimate time of death fitted to that.

They just had to cross-reference this and the fingerprints on the lemonade can for the legal people later in the wrapping up of who gets charged with what. They suspected Tommy's anger hadn't dissipated when he gone round to Daniella's later that week.

They knew that Manny had kept a variety of drugs in his office, thank the sniffer dogs for that discovery, and it was possible that Tommy had taken the lot, hence his actions. Tommy's post mortem supported that drug part. Oliver told Holly that Dan had fought back. She had won that round.

What the police didn't know then, however, was that the security cameras at Daniella's home were linked to the ones in her gym as well as the coffee shop, and she had a full-time guard employed to watch the comings and goings at every property.

Her years in the military made her more aware than regular people of how nothing is to be taken for granted. Her trustworthy guard had seen Tommy at the door to her flat, watching this live feed as Daniella let him in. Then, using the only internal camera, which was positioned to view the hallway and the one that Daniella had activated earlier, he watched as Tommy shoved her violently into the sitting room, causing her to stumble, and thrust a knife, twice, into her stomach.

Immediately calling the emergency services and while waiting on their prompt arrival, her employee continued to watch the horror unfolding, ensuring the record option was functioning as he captured

Daniella move swiftly and using her right leg to deliver a huge kick right into Tommy's stoned face. Tommy was tall but Daniella was faster. And much fitter.

He dropped awkwardly, catching his head on the bookshelf, and she took advantage of this by delivering the killer blow to his neck with her elbow, grabbing his arms forcefully to bend behind his back, and in doing so deliberately breaking one and popping them both out of the sockets, for good measure.

She hogtied him with the sleeves of her bloodied cardigan, and while the sirens were getting closer, she slid down her wall, pushing her blouse into her wounds, and calmly watched him die.

She was rushed to hospital with serious stab wounds, and the last part of the security footage, the unnecessary violence, was deleted by her loyal employee.

He wasn't going to implicate Daniella, as much as she may have gone totally overboard.

Tommy had been intent on taking all of his anger out on his confidante.

And Tommy should have known better than to confront a trained killer.

HOLLY ALSO LOVES A FIGHT

I went to visit Daniella as soon as the hospital authorities allowed me to, and immediately upgraded her to a private suite, as well as installing her own dedicated private nurses as soon as I saw the state she was in.

I had taken locally-bought but out-of-any-UK-season, fat, long grapes, *Sweet Sapphire*, flown in from the USA and pre-washed in my fancy water filter thing that had really wound up the gorgeous Inspector, for some reason. I ate them all when sitting next to her. Spitting the stalks and tough skins back into the paper bag. 'Tinker, tailer, soldier' I sang to her.

She had lost a lot of blood from the first stab wound, and looked really awful. I told her this and she attempted a weak smile when I tried to brush her tangled fringe.

She was hooked up to so many humming and bleeping machines, and she looked very pale and haunted, and when I finally plucked up my own courage to ask her if she really was okay, she said she actually didn't think she was. Which was totally not my Daniella.

And everything hurts now. Everyone lies, some tell white lies. Some make up their past in order not to hurt others, and others enhance their lives at the expense of others. A white lie is a good lie. Susie used to tell me that often. As if she'd have known the difference.

But then, no-one ever shows themselves, their true colours, to anyone, including themselves. Because we can't afford to.

We are scared to. And I think that's because we don't truly understand ourselves, or why we do things, or why we allow those things to continue to give us pain. There's a kind of comfort in that.

I sensed Daniella felt some remorse over Tommy, they had formed some mad bond after Iain's overdose, maybe killing someone you cared for isn't too easy to recover from.

I left her bedside later that first evening, as she had fallen back into a deep drug-induced sleep while I was still holding her as close as I could, kissing her blood matted hair often, noticing her roots desperately needed doing.

I'll tell her that tomorrow. The doctors had assured me that she was steady and strong and doing well and would be back on her own feet very soon, but I was starting to doubt their confidences.

She used to be my strong, solid girlfriend and she kept my world turning. And now she had lost the key to her own starter motor. At least, that's what I said to her on a later visit. I also told her many times not to dare leave me. I told her that I loved her and she smiled at that and said it was about bloody time.

She had just been trying to protect me, she said, but I had known all along about Iain and Susie. I was just waiting to see how Susie would spin it in her famous but typically anticlimactic Will reading.

Susie had bottled it of course, always the most disappointing guest of honour, even at her own last and pathetic pity party.

And that time when Harry thought she was helping me by dropping a massive hint with her wedding video; what an idiot. It made me smile on the inside. Her attempts at trying to get me to understand Susie's actions and for me to get 'to the truth myself' were amateurish and juvenile and futile. Bless her though. She had tried so many times to get me to talk my relationship through with Susie. I was already the head coach in their ridiculous little game you see.

When Iain's shirts came to the wash-basket with her fake *Chanel* 22 body spray sprayed all over, I knew every time that the pathetic pair of them had planned it. The stupid little ways of thinking they were getting one over me. Getting back at me for not divorcing Iain until I had fleeced him of everything. Every dirty penny, they thought.

Though I never really understood Susie's role in that relationship. He was never going to marry her, he had always said she was far too common. And he was never that brilliant in bed either. Or out of it, once I'd snared him. I've really no idea what hold she had over him.

Oh, and that thing about me and the *Sidamo* coffee bean conversation starter? Well, I'd been trying to find something on him to get him to notice me as a woman. I knew he was loaded. When my team were doing the regular internal staff audits, I saw from his personal accounts that he paid Lloyds a hefty wedge of money every month for his imports.

A friend at that Bank told me the commissions they got as a result of this long-standing, regular, unchecked coffee consignment, and then I just knew he was going to be moulded into the man of my dreams.
Because it's not easy being poor, I can tell you.
So why did I stay with my mega-rich mentor of a husband and apparently suffer the bruises?

Two things sister: I'll shout it again:

IT'S ABOUT THE MONEY.

Oh, and secondly, more importantly – without exception, I always got the first punch in.

LETTER FROM AMERICA, NOT SENT

My lovely Holly, if it's not too late I need to share
something with you, and I confess I am such a
coward for not having done this sooner. In the month
after Susie died, I came back over to see my sister –
long after I should have done.
She killed herself, pretty soon after Daniella and her
FBI agent went to visit her, but you won't know that.
They went to get something on me, and I believe
they found it. I'm guessing the agent must have felt
some sort of responsibility for her suicide, as he paid
for her funeral. There's a stone pot dedicated to her
in a field masquerading as a churchyard extension.
He gave me the directions, after giving me the news
of her death, and I went to give my respects.
It's a ramshackle old burial ground next to an
abandoned plantation. Ironic really. The ghosts from
the last few buildings still standing join with me in my
guilt and haunt me in my weakest moments, even
now.
The tumbleweeds form structures higher that you,
and more boring than me you would have said.
In the dusty old container, holding more stones than
loam, I planted some rosemary, for love and
remembrance, even though I met her only the once.
My eyes are stinging in guilt even now, for the
terrible short life she had.
Abandoned by our mother, rejected by her new
family – miles away from her country of birth, and
then discarded by her husband.
Forgotten by me as soon as I got back to England.

Distracted by Susie's almost perfect lies, and my desperate need for an excuse to protect myself from my own disgraceful behaviour. Did my actions drive her suicide?

I picture you with me every night, holding you close, feeling your tiny frame through all of your many protective layers, and I think about what I would have said to you.

Why I've left her husband to rot in jail until he gets the injection. I could have talked to you about my reasons for not telling mum, when she was still alive, that I'd found her daughter, or about a grandchild she never got to meet, and you would have understood while putting me straight.

Making everything okay again. I am sure.

I once tried talking to Susie about this, but she was busy with our wedding – and with the wet ink still drying on my last divorce. I may have attempted this once more but there was never a right moment.

She swept me away. But then there was you.

I didn't always know I was in love with you. I used to leave the room on the rare occasions I was at home when you came round. You did something to me.

I watched you both, unobserved – not in a creepy way I promise. You were so different. I could listen and would compare the two of you and I would punish myself for not speaking out loud a lot earlier. And I felt a fool for having let myself be pushed into something with Susie. I'd actually spoken with her many times, arguments towards the end, about our hasty marriage, and how I wasn't sure it was right for me.

And now that memory weighs heavy in my heart too. And I am really sorry about the tree. I did keep some *Greasy Pippin* seeds you know. I will plant a few for my sister over here, really get to confuse the biodiversity and the indigenous varieties, you will be livid with me for doing so, but if gets you to jump on the next plane I can live with that! I am beyond being rational. I know you always thought I was a daft old block-head, and you were right.

Which person in their right mind would have framed if not an innocent man, but a man not guilty of this particular crime.

I won't tell you any of this though. I thought that was the big secret she had planned to share with us at the Will reading, part two. And I wonder why she didn't. I ask myself, why would anybody want to destroy anyone else? What drove Susie to carry on bullying from beyond the grave?

So, anyway, I'll carry my guilt for a while longer because to share it may push you away from me. And I'll crack on over here, for a little more time, looking at feet, ignoring the freshers' attention – and those of their mums, and grans. I hope I can hear you laughing.

And I also hope that one day soon we'll meet again and explain to each other what really happened, and we'll finally understand it all. Until then I continue to dream that you will come over to me. And marry me, because you want to. I don't want anyone else Holly. It was always you.

ONE ENDING.

Little Holly Hastings, lost in a game that's no longer hers.

AFTERWARDS

Just in case you're interested, the Law Society's solicitor, Samuel Hillary, hadn't in fact slept with Susie. His preference was Manlafi Sarr. And even after he'd had to let Manny go from this particular partnership, they had stayed constant companions and used to push business to each other and, on occasion, revel in the many stories about Hastings and how they had both had kept his commercial undertakings without his knowledge of the other's interactions. So they thought. They were the fun times. It was Manny who told Samuel about Susie's tragic accident after finding this out from his wife.

On the day Mr Hillary's long time, but still trainee, legal-secretary handed in her resignation letter, she confessed to her employer that in the files she had prepared for Susie's second Will reading earlier that year, there may have been an oversight; something possibly had been mislaid.

The single mum, overworked due to the ridiculous demands made on her with both the long hours at work and the extra-curricular activities the school insisted upon for her children, was also terribly underpaid and prone to carelessness.

In view of this exhaustion, she had understandably misfiled a rather large hand-written manilla envelope addressed to Holly.

She remembered, much later, that this had been marked *Private and Confidential* but was to be opened at the second reading by Ms Holly Hastings, the beneficiary, herself.

When the worn-out mother finally found the envelope, some five months later, filed with papers or something kept for Iain Hastings, again not in the right place and which should have been sent with the remainder of the Estate papers, she decided not to immediately tell the senior partner.

The smart woman secured another job first, as a fraud researcher for the Police. Not only was this nearer to her children's school, it was much better pay, shorter hours and something she had always wanted to do – following the money sources of the rich and the corrupt.

She re-filed the papers belonging to Iain Hastings into another dead client's account, as she didn't need to own up to both of those errors.

Being a complete arse, Mr Hillary let his secretary go straight away, without any repercussions, and no time to empty her desk nor the pay she was owed in lieu of the notice period.

And as he sat at his mahogany polished antique desk, the view over the rolling hills of the once-proud industrial heart of this second city, with his own heart saddened with all the recent upsets, he picked the package up from his in-tray.

With this hot potato in his possession, as it now couldn't not be, he turned it over and over and front to back, weighing up the options whilst waiting for the contents to miraculously reveal themselves. Without the need for his involvement.

On the one hand, this may make his firm appear negligent and he couldn't risk being sued.

On the other, it belonged to Holly and whatever the content was, it wasn't his to keep, said the coward to himself, to protect the other partners.

And on top of all of that he couldn't know if his last secretary would spill the beans, should he destroy it. With hindsight, he ought to have dealt with her resignation a lot better. A present, some extra bonus. A bribe. Such wonderful hindsight. Perfectly good 20/20 vision.

Not for this man.

After much deliberation, as was the proper way for any good lawyer to behave, he left the package locked in his private drawer for that whole weekend whilst he decided what to do.

A nasty dose of the latest coronavirus mutation had laid him up for a further two weeks, and then his doctor prescribed some sunshine to help with the recuperation.

Returning to his office just over a month later, his foreign sun tan topped up along with a little botox round the mouth, he knew that in order to make an informed decision he had little option but to open the package. And in addition, he was also a little bit nosey. Who wouldn't have been?

Mr Hillary left this onerous task until the end of the day after attending to his more important clients' emails first, and securing himself a new temp until he could replace the useless and scatty single parent.

Susie's hand-written letter had started:
'Hey, Gold-Digga, you thought he didn't know' and
enclosed with many sheets of vitriolic and nasty
accusations was a backup stick (he didn't load this
up for fear of infecting the law firm's network with
any viruses). There were lots of photographs of
Susie and Iain on their many excursions displaying
such physical prowess, at their age too; shocking
enough to make this solicitor shudder. And he'd had
many booty calls with Manny Sarr.
There was a hard copy of a spreadsheet detailed
with all of Holly's various money trails, the initial
investments in a flower farm in Africa, suggested by
Iain before their marriage, and the ones afterwards
showing excellent results. She was a good pupil.
With most of her companies lodged in Delaware,
those faceless significant controllers leading up to
her Trusts, this was a clever bit of layering.
Regardless, the accumulation and domination
calculations would almost certainly point back to
Holly.
Also in the package were the supporting documents,
perhaps copies, showing the careful laundering of all
this dirty money and how it became sanitised into
her estate.
If this came to light then every single penny Holly
had earned, and inherited, would be reclaimed by
the various fraud squads, internationally, and very
publicly, and she would go to jail.
Plus the solicitor's partnership would suffer greatly,
having not attended to this detail in a timely manner
and reported her.

Susie ended this letter with 'Pillow talk, little Holly. You built your secret empire on dirty money, Iain was going to confront you with this, to stop you getting access to any of his money, and he was going to go after your funds too, he said then he could marry me. Did you ever realise that Abby and Tommy are his? We've sent copies to Manny Sarr, and upon my death you're going to be busted anyway! Just wait until that shit hits the fan. And you always thought I was the loser'.

Quite sure now of the best way to proceed, the cowardly little man asked his foreign cleaner, on that very night, to write Holly's address onto a new plain padded manilla envelope that he had sent his temp out to buy at lunchtime.

With absolutely nothing to suggest it had come from his office. The old leftover Christmas stamps from a petty cash tin, pre-glued, attached by the same cleaner, no spit from him, would ensure no trace of any company-specific franking machine ink-stamp. Mr Hillary decided he would post the evidence from a faraway location the following weekend, and rid himself of everything for good.

As with all undervalued secretaries who knew they were going to get shafted, this one hadn't bothered to update Holly's records, as, in her mind, there was no legal requirement to do so.

Holly wasn't their client. As a result, the incriminating evidence was sent to Holly's old house. Holly hadn't set any postal forwarding addresses up, mostly because she hadn't thought about it, and so any mail or dusty old advertising flyers still sat in the post box at her old house, within the once-fancy gated community.

The housing development was being pulled down due to the planning permission departments' recent lawsuit about taking hefty bungs to allow the building on contaminated land, and in their haste to put things right and secure the vote for the other side in the next local election, no-one thought to check the mail boxes before sending the bulldozers in.

It was always about the money.

COMING SOON

OTHER PEOPLE'S GHOSTS

OTHER PEOPLE'S GHOSTS

Most days I like to sit on my bench in the park next to the seaside, while waiting for my wife to hurry up. There's a new, very tall lady sat on a lavender bench just further up, on the opposite side of the walkway. She hasn't said hello, but I think that's because the sun is in her eyes. Maybe she hasn't got her orientation yet.

Two seats further up, an older lady. She has been coming here a long time, even before me, I think she said. Sometimes she's joined by a much older man who pats his pockets looking for cigarettes as he attempts to sit next to her. She always moves away. She's very sad and keeps looking over to the new girl.

I don't know when the workmen come to give the benches a new lick of paint, but they're always dry by the time we all get here.

The many trees that hide the sand also protect some people, who aren't ready to come out onto the bright benches. I've never been in that area, but I've glimpsed some people, and heard a lot of sobbing. Some familiar faces are making their way to the dedicated seats; we always manage to get our usual.

When we notice one of the regulars doesn't visit anymore, that's when their benches get repainted and then we know we have a new person ready to embrace the wonderful new scenery.

I am keeping an eye on the older lady, the one that is so desperate to talk to the lavender girl.

She brings a huge handbag with her every day and sorts through her trinkets one by one, sometimes she puts them onto the bench next to her. She never cries. I think she's a tough old bird to be honest. Not like my wife.

There's a young lad too. He started coming before the lavender girl. He was in a right old state to begin with, but the fresh air seems to have done him good. I think he has come to look for his mother, but we've not noticed anyone fitting her description. He has a dark brown seat very close to the edge of the trees. He's not here every day.

I raise my face to the sun and imagine I can hear my wife. She must be on her way soon. Only so many motherly things she can still be doing.

The old lady has left a trinket on her light blue seat and she's just walked past our newest companion. She hasn't said anything to her, but the younger lady looks up at her, and when she has past, she goes over to the empty seat and picks up the trinket. From here it looks like a war medal, but I can't be sure.

The lavender girl moves past the young lad and he looks up at her as though he knows her, but drops his head back down quickly.

The little black Cocker Spaniel, the one with the wonky smile who comes and visits the new people, comes over to see how I am. 'Fine' I tell her. She sits with me for a while.

The warm wind stirs up the sea and I think about taking a walk down to the beach. I've not got that far yet, but as I don't want to miss the wife, I stay firmly put on my turquoise seat and open the newspaper.

I've witnessed these scenes so often. They always unfurl, with the right results, but I have a feeling this new group has a lot to understand. Not that I can help with that.
But other people can.